M000104763

Winter's Song
A Hymn to the North

— TD Mischke —

Skywater Publishing Cooperative
Chaska, Minnesota
https://lskywaterpub.com

Library of Congress Control Number: 2023938282
    ISBN: 978-1-0881-1647-0 (Ingram hardcover)
    ISBN: 978-1-0881-3258-6 (Ingram paperback)
    ISBN: 978-1-0881-1655-5 (Ingram ebook)

Credits
Connie R. Colwell, editorial direction
Flat Sole Studio, cover design and book layout

Photo Credits
Minnesota Historical Society, front cover
Wilson Webb, back cover

"It is the life of the crystal, the architect of the flake, the fire of the frost, the soul of the sunbeam. This crisp winter air is full of it."
— **John Burroughs, naturalist**

To Rosie,

In the snow-covered cabin,
with the book, by the fire,
laughing at the howling wind.

Contents

Introduction

"It has been ordained that there be summer and winter, abundance and dearth, virtue and vice, and all such opposites for the harmony of the whole."
— **Epictetus, Greek philosopher**

It's a sprawling, sunlit, late summer afternoon and the world is a parade of flourishing life, some of it buzzing near the screen door, some of it soaring through happy blue skies, some scurrying across shady lawns, some posing and posturing in garden beds. The singing trees form a canopy over the neighborhood streets as shy, giggling children sell lemonade in plastic cups, calling out to those drifting past, walking their dogs, delivering newspapers, jogging, or strolling arm in arm.

There's a ballgame on the radio, and a stooped, wiry, gray-haired man washes his car with a garden hose as he listens. A motorcycle engine revs in the distance, and an ice cream truck speaker counters with high notes that resemble wind chimes.

Winter is absent from the minds of all who are found here. It rests in a distant galaxy. The very idea of it couldn't seem more foreign. It's not possible to fathom in this world of radiant abundance, held softly in a cradle of warm, humid air.

The weather makes many feel lazy. On porches, people can be seen sitting alone or in pairs. Some read, some quietly stare, some talk to children in their yards. As much as possible the town has moved outdoors. The languid afternoon calls everyone within range to step into the July air and bask in this sun-soaked showcase. Those stuck indoors feel a familiar anxiety as an idyllic day slips past while they tackle obligations and responsibilities they're yearning to discard, feeling a restless child inside longing to race across an open field, barefoot, or barrel down a cedar dock out into the weightless air, over a lake as blue as the heavens.

A young couple walks by, waving to a neighbor. The combined weight of their clothing wouldn't match that of a single winter boot. The thin cotton rests atop their skin as if only lighting upon it momentarily. Their bare shoulders glisten and court the sunshine.

The thrill of playing hooky is born of days like this, be it skipping school, a job, or just failing to show up to help a relative move, sensing that summer is too short to give up these precious hours hauling boxes.

Months from now, on a frigid, snowy January day, some of those here will close their eyes and allow this scene to reappear in their mind's eye. It won't stay long; it will flash as some image on a postcard, then fade. But the strange sensation of the contrast it presents will linger, and the question might be asked, is this really the same neighborhood? Is this even the same planet?

This is a book about that other world, winter. It addresses the intimate relationship between the season and those people in the U.S. who confront it, or embrace it, struggle with it, or waltz with it. Where there is true winter, in the northern states, far from the two coasts, there are countless numbers of people who have been molded by those cold months, shaped by them, taught, tamed, and trained by them.

I have been all over the hard winter region of the lower 48 states in America. Whether I'm in Northern Michigan, Wisconsin, Minnesota, the Dakotas, or Eastern Montana, there is a shared winter language and winter culture. There can be variations in the season's intensity, but there is far more similarity in the way these people have come to understand and interact with this otherworldly presence, a force that does its best to lay claim to the largest chunk of the calendar.

In this book, I will treat these areas as one location, one state onto itself, winter's hometown. And the people I will introduce to you will be presented as citizens of a single territory. Which city they reside in will be unimportant. They are Northerners, and in terms of winter they speak the same language, know the same touchstones, and share much of the same nuanced understanding.

In the North, winter will not be ignored. If you've made your home where winter rules, you've been forced to develop some type of relationship with this phenomenon. But this book is about more than the season and its relationship to people. It's a hymn to the connection between winter and the ineffable, mysterious experience of our very existence. It celebrates the ways the season weaves its way into every facet of what it is to be alive.

In these pages, I will attempt to examine winter through my own experiences, the experiences of others, and sometimes through the viewpoints of people who exist only in my mind. It's my hope that, by the end of this book, you will come to appreciate the season from a new and fresh perspective. If you have never known a true Northern winter, I'm honored to be the one to throw open the curtain. And if you already live it, season after season, take a walk with me through a familiar world, so I might share these stories with a kindred spirit.

The Gateway

"Wisdom comes with winters."
— **Oscar Wilde**

It looms. I can't see it yet, but in that first week of November, it looms. I sense it, marching toward me, like an old relative on a lumbering trek from a distant town, some brooding uncle who will dominate a table gathering without uttering a word just by the weight of his presence.

Each year, I anticipate our impending visitor, and each year I feel that familiar rush of sensations. Nostalgia, wistfulness, wonder, resignation, and old joy, they all roll through me, and I instinctively make the necessary internal adjustments.

Some Northerners start to prepare, psychologically, when that first cool autumn wind blows in September. They're already grieving summer's end and lamenting all that awaits. Not me. Summer in the North passes like a languid dream, and I heartily welcome the glorious autumn, with its explosion of color and its short but clarion song. It's only after Halloween that I pick up the vibrational shift and take note of that familiar relative on the horizon beginning that steely march.

Here is the boundary between greeting and farewell. The greeting feels ancient and inevitable. And the goodbye has an elegiac weight. It holds the mournful reminder of life's brevity, the grief inherent in all existence, the way time is pulling me along and always has been. While I've been attending to all that must be attended to, the clock has been steadily advancing beside me, never slowing, never resting, never caring about circumstance, no mercy, just a stoic stroll toward an eventual end. Winter is the reminder that it all dies—all of it.

Winter is a hymn to what it is to be human. Nature goes dormant, color disappears from the landscape. But in that mysterious desolation, there rises stark beauty. The season has become a kind of bible, a Northerner's Dead Sea scroll. It teaches about going inward, about facing the dark, about learning to take on what life throws at us with a willingness to be game for it all, not just the easy stuff. It teaches patience. It teaches that, just as the finest way to enjoy the warmth of a fire in a hearth is to have known the biting cold, we cannot know pleasure without suffering, we cannot know the beauty of love without having known its absence.

Winter brims with more wisdom than can be absorbed in a single season. So those seasons repeat. And, over the years, we Northerners wear those seasonal lessons on our weathered faces, and one can soon come to distinguish those of the North from those living in warm climates. Absent is that light glow that comes with a Californian's illusions. In its place are the creases of a Northerner's realism, accompanied by a wry smile that says, in the end we all die, anyway, so pour that hot toddy, and let's watch the snowfall.

Elsewhere in the country, others will claim to have winter. In fact, they'll say winter is a season in every state; it merely varies in presentation. But I can't listen to that. I don't have it in me to empathize. We here in the North have winter and they don't, end of story.

And if the Northern winter delivers its first soulful prelude in early November, its first formal missive, announcing its imminent arrival is the conclusion of daylight saving time, when all clocks "fall back." As children we memorized "fall back and spring forward" as the way to remember which way to turn our time piece. And "fall back" could not be a more apt description for what happens in November. The clock falls back whence it came as if settling into its true home. And I let go and fall back into who I am as a Northerner.

November plays with the clock and plays with the light. It has its own glow. Look at the windows the sun enters, the new angles, that particular quality of late-afternoon illumination, the time of day when this bookshelf is now graced, when that couch glows softly. Those items didn't know sunlight before, but it's November, everything's shifting.

November is a neglected month. People skip over it when listing the significant months stamped in their memories: the sweet promise of April and May, the orgiastic dance of October, the top 40 hits of June, July, and August, sacred December, and bitter January.

Although November is treated as a second-rate month, it's bursting with stories and dirges, and the older I get the more I'm game to listen. November is a month for the poet. It's the pensive pause between seasons. It's when I walk outside and feel the grass under my feet, yet the ground is hard as stone. The trees are not yet filled with hoarfrost, but they are empty of leaves. Their stark crooked arms reach hauntingly into the dimming light of a late-afternoon scarlet sky. There is a yearning in that silhouette, or maybe a salutation to the transcendent wonder of it all. I imagine writers at their windows earnestly staring at this tableau tinged with pathos. How could they not be inspired to pen a fervent paean?

November is a month of palpable expectation. I think back on summer and remember an enchantress whose spell I fell under for a dizzying drunken stretch. But that's all behind me now. I'm being called back home to mother.

Southerners visiting the North Country in November sample the air and claim winter has already arrived, but they are of another clan and speak a different language. November is not winter. It's merely unlocking the gate. The winter label belongs to December, January, February, and March. If numbing cold and snow slip in a little earlier in the year, or stay a little later, this doesn't change the fundamental reality. It's like throwing a football in July or trick-or-treating an hour before dark on Halloween. You're playing with expectations, that's all. Winter does that too. But December, January, February, and March are the certified, stamped, and formally packaged months of winter. They each have their own feel, and their own unique characteristics.

But don't trust their personality traits when described by those who aren't Northerners. Winter, in much of the national conversation, gets shoddy treatment. It's dismissed with throwaway lines that are weak and lightweight. When traveling, you tell someone where you're from and you hear, "It's nice up there in the summer." It's the well-trodden, seven-word backhanded compliment that leaves silent its final seven: "But, how do you stand the cold?"

Of course, you don't have to travel to hear this. In the Northland, you'll always find some people who talk of "getting out." It's brought up the way one might speak of a prison furlough. Spring is pined for, summer is Shangri-La, autumn is listed as many people's favorite season. But winter? Winter is too often spoken of as though it's to be tolerated at best. I question the Northern credentials of these grumblers. They've been spoiled by skyways, domed stadiums, indoor golf ranges, mega malls, and underground heated garages. They've joined the group that lives through the season in denial. With them, the cold is not to be faced and embraced, it's to be chased and erased. Yet, we're talking about a third of our lives here. Winter doesn't just slip in for a cup of coffee; it dominates. Failing to explore what all it is, and what gifts it can deliver, gifts the Southern world will never know, is like acknowledging that sleep consumes a third of our lives but never being curious about dreams.

One gift winter offers is the way it slows down time. And I, like many, need to slow the frenzied clock of an overstuffed life. Winter's restfulness follows the swirl of fall, that preparation for the coming cold, the caring for plants and gardens, removing dead leaves, winterizing windows, throwing plastic sheets around back porches, storing patio furniture, cleaning gutters, stacking firewood, tuning up snow blowers, and for some old-schoolers, swapping the screen windows for those heavy wooden storms.

For me, winter signals it's time to move inward, and it brings its own shift in daydreams. There are longer stretches of introspection, and weightier thoughts. It's like the difference between a summer afternoon with friends and the wee hours of a summer night alone. Summer afternoons are for seeing what I can do, its late nights are for asking who I am. Such is the stark difference between July and January. They have little in common. And to roll with that, to learn to roll with that, is the rich byproduct of maturity. How many of us spend our lives fighting change, the one unshakable constant of existence. Winter tells me to give up the fight. I could move to Florida and imagine life as one long summer day, but why delude myself? Winter invites me to learn of life's deeper truths, and in so doing, to learn who I am, part of a natural dance, one that's pulling me along to some mystifying and sacred beat. I'm a complex and fleeting soul passing through time like a north wind moving across the prairie. Winter asks me to let go and trust the natural forces that brought me here in the first place.

First Snow

"Winter is not a season, it's a celebration."
— **Anamika Mishra, author and travel blogger**

There are two distinct experiences of a "First Snow." One is the first snowfall Northerners experience at the beginning of each winter season. The second is the snow experienced by someone moving to the Northland and taking in winter for the very first time, having grown up in a climate that never offered such a vista. They are separate and unrelated experiences, unique unto themselves.

For Northerners, the first snow each year seems as fresh and novel and filled with surprise and wonder as the first snowfall the year before, or the year before that. The months of spring, summer, and fall bring a seasonal amnesia. By the time November rolls around again, the experience of the last winter is practically forgotten. The weight of it is no longer felt. It's been stripped away by the glory of spring's thaw, the baking heat of summer, and the idyllic conditions of autumn. The slate has been wiped clean. I'm able to look at that first snow like I did as a child. It's dazzling and magnificent the way the sky can send billions of fluffy white visitors of such ethereal beauty to gracefully decorate the lonely, outstretched branches and embrace the withering brown turf with something so soft, pure, and pristine. In a matter of hours all is transformed, a new planet has appeared, and the metamorphosis is breathtaking.

But, as with the arrival of winter itself, there is always that vague accompanying grief. The grass that's been stared at for months will be seen no more, not till well into the next year. I've walked on it, lain on it, ditched sidewalks just to feel it beneath me, I've stared at it from the window of the car, yard after yard offering a stately green welcome mat for every house. I've cut it, raked it, and taken note of the way it complements every tree, shrub, bush, or flower. And now it's gone. Oh, it's there, of course, beneath the snow, but so is the sun behind the clouds on misty gray days. It doesn't change the sense of it having vanished. In this case, for a long, long time.

Every Northerner knows what it's like to walk over to the window and stare out at that first snowfall, letting all the memories, mixed emotions, and random musings parade through the head and the heart. I spend more time at the window with that first snow than with any snowfall that follows. The first snow is evocative in a way that can be compared to the first thunderstorm of spring, which also brings familiar sensations that have not been felt in many months. They've been forgotten in that same seasonal amnesia.

Spring, summer, and fall creep up. There's a slow unfolding with each of those seasons. No one can say when exactly summer arrives, or when fall is truly here, or on what day spring is suddenly in our midst. But the first snow has a way of removing autumn in one dramatic yank of the stage curtain. Instantly, the new season is here. No matter how barren the landscape was before that first snow, it still had the appearance of late autumn. When the first snow descends, winter is introduced dramatically. No other season comes along in such an audacious manner. Winter seems determined from the get-go to let Northerners know it's a season unlike the rest. It doesn't knock gently on the front door; it kicks it down.

And when the snow is fresh and new, so too is life. I'm shaken awake. Change is something I too often don't realize I need until I get it, but without it, I slip into routine, and too much routine leads to sleepwalking. Leave the house after the first snow, however, and walk into a restaurant, coffee shop, or bar, and everyone is carrying a palpable new energy, operating at a slightly different frequency. We're all morphing into winter people, and I can't help but feel slightly more alive, trying on this distinct identity. It gives me my sense of place. Here I am back in a familiar setting, the one that separates Northerners from other parts of the country. I move forward with quiet confidence and a vague hint of pride. I know how to do this. For better or worse, I am home.

But there is a second type of first snow, one that is even more dramatic for those experiencing it, and that's the first snow of one's life. If born here, Northerners cannot remember the moment they first experienced snow. But, if arriving here later in life, from a tropical climate, it's something a person can talk about with wide-eyed wonder.

Some immigrants from tropical regions exhibit a slack-jawed astonishment that native Northerners will never know. I have often wondered if that experience is akin to the one I had as a child when I first went up in an airplane and could not believe I was inside a cloud, clouds I had only known from an impossible distance. It all seemed to be occurring in a kind of dream. The world had not prepared me for this moment. Is it like that for those experiencing their first snow, after a lifetime of knowing nothing but lush green?

Nannah Kjos grew up in Manilla where she had never seen snow. She moved to Minnesota at age 35. On that November day when the snow fell before her for the first time, her reaction was uncontrollable giggling. She asked people around her, "Is this it? Is this really it? Is this snow?" She said a little-kid energy surged through her and she ran around deliriously.

"I was with some friends who had also just arrived from Asia. We were racing around laughing uncontrollably. We felt so much joy. We were taking out our phones and recording it, recording each other. We were sticking out our tongues and tasting it. We couldn't believe how soft it was. We had all expected it to be like the ice chips in a snow cone."

When all the snow had fallen and covered the land completely, Nannah said she stood and stared at it with astonishment. "When I looked out at that white world, I actually cried. I cried at the beauty of it. It was the most wonderful thing I had ever seen in my life. It overwhelmed me."

Thereafter, whenever it snowed, Nannah would take photos of the fresh pristine scene and send the photos home to Asia, always with the same words: "So white, so beautiful, so quiet, so cold." She said she always made sure to include a description of the "quiet," because after each snowfall that was what struck her most, when she stepped outside, the remarkable quiet of the world around her.

In the ensuing weeks, sights Northerners took for granted were unfathomable to Nannah. Like the notion of a lake freezing solid. She said she couldn't understand how such a thing was possible. She would stare at lakes and watch people walk on the ice, and she'd marvel.

"I thought they were so brave. How can they do this and trust that they won't fall through? I sent pictures back to Asia and people there could hardly believe their eyes."

On a trip with her new husband to Northern Minnesota, Nannah had the scare of her life, and thrill of her life, all in a single activity. Her husband drove their vehicle onto a frozen lake. She said it was one thing for her to watch people walk on the ice, but to drive on it seemed like a death wish.

"He was driving so fast and turning the wheel and spinning us around and around. I was crying I was so scared. I was sure the lake was going to swallow us up. I was sure I was going to die. But I also found myself laughing. I was crying and I was laughing at the same time, because it was both so scary and so thrilling, and also so strange. I just kept crying and laughing. I wanted desperately to get off the ice, but part of me wanted him to keep doing it, to feel the scariness, like a thrill ride at a carnival."

Of course, many from tropical climates are more intimidated by the cold and snow than they are enthralled. Pata Simpson grew up in Jamaica and experienced the winters of the North Country for the first time at the age of 44. His first reaction to a world covered in white was that this was going to be an environmental disaster.

"I said, all of these trees are going to die, every one of them are going to die. I cannot live where there will be no trees. And these will not make it."

He had to be reassured by several locals that the trees of the North would be just fine, and would green up again come spring, but he found this impossible to believe.

Alfreda Daniels came from Liberia and told me that the first time she saw snow it just felt all wrong.

"That was the word that came to mind. I just thought there was something wrong with a world like this. I thought to myself, a person does not go outside in this. Why are people outside at all, why are people driving? I honestly did not understand how a person was supposed to survive in this. In fact, the day I arrived in America there was snow on the ground and within minutes of arriving I had slipped and fallen and hurt myself. That was my introduction to snow, that you just fall down all the time and get hurt."

Chiqui Rosales de Ryan had a very different take. She felt a reverence for what she was witnessing. Emigrating to the Northland from Guatemala, she encountered her first snowfall in her early 20s. But it wasn't just any snowfall. It was the infamous Halloween blizzard of 1991, which dumped 28 inches of snow on the Minneapolis-Saint Paul metro area. "I kept looking up in the sky, over and over again, trying to see where it was all coming from," she said, as if hoping to discover a cosmic bucket that had been tipped on its side. "But then I just realized it is coming from God. This is God's creation. And right then I felt a sense of awe."

Tati Unga ran out into his first snowfall barefoot. He had seen snow on TV, and on the movie screen, back in Tonga, but the screen failed to convey the temperature.

"I ran out there not knowing it would be so cold. I was shocked. I did not know the snow came with such a feeling. I didn't expect that. That first winter I did everything wrong. I was given thermal underwear, and I wore it on the outside of my clothes because I did not know any better. People all laughed at me. It took me a while to figure out how to live in this world."

To view winter through the eyes of these newcomers is to see it fresh once more, and to wake up that part of oneself that needs prodding and poking from time to time. We learn once again that experience is dependent on our frame of reference. Nature does what she does over and over again, season after season, but what we bring to our window is a constantly shifting confluence of age, experience, emotion, and perspective. Winter has taught me that, ultimately, each of us will decide on our own what the season will be called. It has no stake in the matter. It has no name. We are the ones making it a gift, or a thrill, or some ethereal mystery to be pondered, or drudgery to be endured. Winter has no words, only the dance. And we are invited to the ball, to either study it from the shadows or join it under the dizzying lights, letting it lead, and take us where it will.

Tuck's Winter Tour

"Winter, a lingering season, is a time to gather golden moments and embark upon a sentimental journey."
— **John Boswell, Yale professor**

Just moving in? Well, welcome to the Northland. Call me Tuck. Everyone does. You're a long way from home, Kid. Anyone give you the lowdown? Each person will lay it out a little differently. They say no two snowflakes are alike. Well, no two views of winter are quite the same either. But I have what I believe to be the simplest outline for the coming season if you're up for it; just a quick overview of what all you're in for. It's the brochure they should've given you at the border.

Looking at the calendar, winter is gearing up to introduce herself to you in less than a month, so it's good to get on top of it now. I'll try to make this as concise as possible.

I used to spend a fair amount of time wondering how Thanksgiving, Christmas, and New Year's ended up bundled together in one short five-week stretch that happened to coincide with the first five weeks of winter. But, regardless, the result has been a brilliant diversion to keep people's attention off this long, cold, dark chapter we're entering.

If looming winter lets in a distant whisper just after Halloween, it delivers a welcome holiday respite right at the starting line. And not just any holiday, mind you, one that's synonymous with the warmth of family, filled with expressions of love and gratitude. All this coming right when it might be tempting for some to feel melancholy over the loss of the sun and the long, cold march ahead.

Thanksgiving says, "Hey, don't be getting all gloomy on me now. We've set up a little time off of work for you, as well as an opportunity to relax with relatives around a banquet table, so you can recall all the fine things that have come your way this past year. Pay no attention to the rallying cold and dimming light. Focus on the turkey, and Aunt Kay's parlor games."

The thing is, it works. It's too difficult to see winter's impending gloom when Thanksgiving presents the most popular secular holiday of the year. And the diversions don't let up there. When Thanksgiving's long weekend is over and it's back to work, it's suddenly "The Holiday Season."

"Don't focus on that 4:30 p.m. sunset," the chorus shouts. "Focus on the twinkling colored lights going up on the houses and businesses. Revel in the spirit of giving, that's growing in intensity right alongside that growing darkness. And repeat these lyrics: "City sidewalks, busy sidewalks, dressed in holiday style." Or my favorite line, "Children laughing, people passing, meeting smile after smile…" you know the song.

What's that? You're not a Christian? Me neither, but a slew of different cultures around the world have a sacred and festive take on this time of year. You can substitute anything you like, but the lights and the joy and the music work a kind of magic for most everyone, and the carol, "Silver Bells," spells it out delightfully. Whether artificially manufactured or genuine, the spirit of the holiday season does infect a fair percentage of folks, religious or not. It's contagious, and it creates a palpable energy that gives a boost to the mood.

Anyway, at this point, winter is still brand new. There hasn't been time for it to wear on anyone yet, and the holidays have most everyone focusing attention on house gatherings, toasts, and end-of-the-year office parties. The giddiness can get one thinking back to childhood, and many of those early memories will warm your heart. TV specials will fill the masses with holiday cheer, and the snow outside will tastefully enhance the tableau. The thing is, snow is supposed to be here. An L.A. panorama would be a rank absurdity right now, a harsh affront to the senses. Snow isn't a hardship at this point. It's what we demand for the holidays. It's a Hollywood setting straight out of *It's A Wonderful Life*.

And just about the time Christmas passes, our attention moves on to yet a third bacchanalia. New Year's Eve offers the promise of a fresh start and the completion of something quite monumental, a year in a human life. Suddenly, a new set of thoughts occupies the mind, once again keeping at bay all thoughts of the sinking temperatures and blanketing darkness. Reflections on the year that has passed, and hope for the year to come, pepper conversations. Drinks flow and songs are sung, and the party that started with Thanksgiving Day wraps up with shouts, hugs, kisses, and merry midnight revelry.

For many, that run from Thanksgiving through New Year's Day is a vertiginous, almost dream-like entry into the winter season. But it comes with a bracing bend in the road that leaves one in a wholly different state of mind, come the morning of January 2. A glaring reality drops down with a dull and ominous thud.

I've always described this next stretch of winter as "The Long 90." This is the number of days, give or take, that Northerners will have to trudge through to arrive at that first welcoming spring breeze. And they will be days without significant holiday diversions, and days where winter will not seem so fresh, and they'll include the coldest days of the year. It's a startling come-down from the holiday razzle-dazzle, and it seems to be a major flaw in the grand design. As brilliant as the clustering of Thanksgiving, Christmas, and New Year's was, The Long 90 represents a debacle. There's no kind way to put it: The party's over.

There are three ways people tend to look at the vista staring at them come January 2. Some feel relief. The holidays were just too demanding. Spending time, energy, and money, maintaining the rituals, and keeping up with the festive toasts and glad-handing was just plain exhausting. January presents an opportunity for welcome rest. Like a bear entering a winter den, these people treat the month like a cave to relish, hunkering down and doing very little. In fact, many of us feel we are being given cosmic permission to do very little. We did plenty in December. Too much, some would argue. And it's now the coldest month of the year. It offers the perfect excuse to let the gears grind to a halt and to deliver a giant exhale. The month is tailor-made for inertia, and it's a gift from the gods for any and all introverts.

But there's a second group that views the world from this perch as a wonder to behold, a wild gift to the senses, a playground to enjoy, an inviting contrast to the other seasons. These are people who take full advantage of those winter offerings available no other time of year. They feel lucky to live where such treasure is laid out before them. They're not a crowd your average Hawaiian will understand, but you'll do well to learn from them. They'll overhaul your outlook and readjust your attitude.

Of course, there are plenty who find themselves someplace darker. On January 2 this third group takes on the full weight of winter for the very first time. If they didn't prepare for it, if winter is a season they just try to "get through" on their way to enjoying life on the other side, this moment is the sobering and somber wakeup call. What lies ahead are 90 days of a stark white landscape, bare trees, and arctic air. Ninety days to get to those first mild, sunny April afternoons. Life may be short, and each day may be precious, but to these people the next three months could be skipped entirely if someone had the power to make their life a bit shorter.

I feel for these people. They are not where they belong. The fates have made a blunder placing them here. Phoenix is waiting, and Boca Raton. Corpus Christi is calling, and its sales pitch is echoed by Santa Barbara and Santa Fe. When an entire season in the Northland is viewed as a growling predator outside your window, or a gray-walled prison, it's time to pack up the kids and blow town, like the dustbowl refugees fleeing Oklahoma for California's promised land. The rest of us understand. You have a mindset we've encountered often. We've stopped trying to talk you into a new perspective. We realize there are different types of people on this earth, and some were never meant to be Northlanders. You deserve joy. You deserve to find the climate soulmate you were meant to partner with on this planet.

But if you do stick around, and if you do make it through January, the good news is that the worst is over, my friend.

February is best known for what it's not: January and March. It's not the coldest, harshest month that kicks off every new year, and it's not the last tired strides at the end of a long road. It's the month that firmly separates those who enjoy winter from those who tolerate it.

If you enjoy the outdoors in winter, February will give you plenty of snow and plenty of reasonably mild days—even a lot of sunshine. But if you've been waiting out the winter, it's getting old by now. Your failure to have done more with the season than watch it through a window is starting to take its toll. You thought winter would move faster. But nothing moves fast when you're staring at it. This is when the grudging-toleration crowd can tolerate, grudgingly, no more. If they have the cash and the time, they seek a few sunny days in Miami or San Diego, to give their spirit some defibrillation. And all of these escape artists ask themselves, on that trip, why they don't just live where they're only visiting. Each one will contemplate a move. If not soon, certainly before they die. These are not fun people to hang around on a cold snowy day. They're developing an irritable edge and seem mildly depressed. I've often thought we should have a separate neighborhood just for such residents, a commiseration community with a well-stocked bar.

Now, if you're not part of the grudging-toleration crowd, but find yourself a hearty winter enthusiast, February can be a blissful playground. The days are getting longer, and that growing daylight feels good bouncing off the white. You'll get days below zero at some point in this month, but you'll also see temps above freezing. You'll get little hints that spring is just weeks away and it will fuel you to enjoy the remaining days of winter while you can. You'll make sure you start doing the things you told yourself you'd do more often, way back in November, when giving yourself that winter pep talk. The ice skates will come out, the cross-country skis will slip on, the fishing poles will make it onto the ice, the snowmobile will fire up, or the snowshoes will get a workout. Winter is fleeting, damn it, get out there, there are activities you could be enjoying that you'll never be able to come spring.

The entire season will wrap up with one final sigh come March. You'll damn near smell the looming thaw. So close, yet so far. April is sitting on the flip side of that calendar page, but you're now in the snowiest month of the year, so prepare for spring to seem further away than ever. You've got one thing going for you, however, if you're someone who struggles with the length of the season. You have the start of daylight saving time. This is the extraordinary gift of March. March will bring longer days anyway, just by its placement nine weeks past the winter solstice, but daylight saving time will kick that sun into the sky well after supper, and that's the first thrill of March. Sun in the sky after supper brings an infusion of energy. It is the light shining at the end of a tunnel. Some will ride it blithely, like a Tunnel of Love at an amusement park. Others will ride it like claustrophobics in a mineshaft, but both are feeling the same energetic shift. Spring is arriving soon, a time when the angels will come out to dance like 17-year-olds at the prom, and all of nature will join in choreographed splendor.

There you go, my friend. There's your preview of what's ahead. Get ready. Come at winter with a strategy. Greet it with your arms wide open. Or, if this wakeup call just woke you too harshly, get a condo in Tampa.

Warm & Cozy

"Shut the door, not that it lets in the cold but that it lets out the coziness."
— **Mark Twain**

I'm always intrigued by the way different countries of the world can identify a specific cultural experience deserving of its own special term.

An example is the Russian word *razbliuto*, which refers to the feelings you have toward someone you once loved. I often wonder why there is not a word to describe that in English. Another example is the German word *Kummerspeck*, which, translated, means the weight one gains from overeating due to grief or sadness. Do we see less distressed over-eating on this side of the ocean? Why didn't we label this like the Germans did? Here in the Northland, we've learned of a Danish word that has no one-word English translation, and this one seems inexcusable. *Hygge* is an experience as common to winter life here as the crunch of snow underneath our boots. Yet, the Danes gave it a word, and the English-speaking world did not.

Being cozy, warm, and snug, in an agreeable, intimate environment, enjoying simple pleasures with those closest to you, is one way citizens of the North have gotten through long winters since the invention of those winters. But we need the words "cozy," "warm," and "snug," as well as "agreeable intimate environment," and "enjoying simple pleasures with those closest to us" to get at a full and proper translation of that one five-letter Danish word, *hygge*.

It's doubtful the Danes recognized something we failed to. But it's probably fair to say they elevated its importance by giving it a singular term, and then emphasized it in their culture in a way English speakers did not. I blame the Puritans, or any similar stoic workaholics who pulled their collars up and ventured North with a humorless drive to labor, eat, sleep, and die, praying for a more hospitable world in the afterlife. It's a shame, because *hygge* is an invaluable ticket to taking a season that offers its share of struggle and turning it into one that offers its share of bliss.

Come in from the coldest and darkest of winter nights and encounter candlelight accenting the room and the smell of bread baking in the oven. Look toward the glowing fireplace and see three old friends gathered there, sitting close to one another, pouring a drink, and talking quietly and intimately. You may not know the Danish word *hygge* but you are bathing in it right now. Play a favorite song through those living room speakers and flop down in an overstuffed chair near the window, so you can look out and see the white flakes passing by the streetlight outside. Is your song an old familiar tune that was played in your home when you were young? What's happening to you as you look around the room; what are you feeling? What is it about this moment that is so enhanced by the addition of flame and friends, by the aroma of food being prepared, and the knowledge that this shelter is more than home on this winter night, it's a sacred oasis.

Hygge will carry you through the long, cold dark. It should be prominently featured on any pocket roadmap for navigating the year's harshest season. It comes in a myriad of forms, including oversized sweaters, thick socks, warm blankets, homemade sweets, and hot drinks. But it's also an attitude of appreciation that's felt for the simple things, like reading a book on the couch, knitting by the fireplace, or softly playing an acoustic guitar, no deadlines, no need to do much more than experience the joy of being alive. Maybe it's a walk outside on a night when the holiday lights cover the fronts of houses and the park nearby features children sledding in the moonlight. You come back home all rosy-cheeked and soon find yourself sitting around the dining room table playing a board game with neighbors. All of it falls under the heading of *hygge*. And if it's not making you feel a warm, familiar joy and deep inner peace, keep at it. It'll take you there eventually. One day, spring winds will blow, all the snow will melt, and you won't need it any longer. But you'll know it's waiting there for you next winter, like Grandpa's old lumberjack coat in that antique cedar chest.

You should know that Denmark is consistently ranked as one of the top three happiest places on earth. How much of that can be credited to their emphasis on *hygge* in those winter months? When the citizenry turns winter into something to look forward to, heartily embrace, and make memorable, they display an enviable ability to master their environment, to slant it in their favor. Winter doesn't arrive with emotion, meaning, and insight built into it. We all make of it what we will. The Danes have chosen to make it a wonderland and an opportunity for celebrating life in an enchantingly different way from the rest of the year. Their enduring sense of well-being and contentment is the byproduct. People of the North, all over the globe, would be wise to emulate such a life-affirming perspective.

Winter Window #1

The inside of my house is a radiant photo
Vibrant and vivid
Textured drapes and rugs flaunt and preen
But the window frames a stark black and white
Bare trees, gray skies, snowy rooftops
Indoors, the amber couch is lit
by a dancing fire
framed by ruddy red bricks
But outdoors, warmth is found only in memory
A sick child
home from school
bedroom painted in soft blues and mossy greens
He's staring out a frosted window
Its austere offerings free him to brood
and he curls under his blankets
His mother will bring hot soup
She'll float into the room
wearing a maroon sweater and gold skirt
And the outdoors will seem miles away
Just some vintage black and white
framed on a wall
fading to a ragged memory
in a worn scrapbook
blown open, five decades later
by a single breeze through the heart

It's a Kid's World

"The color of springtime is flowers; the color of winter is in our imagination."
— **Terri Guillemets, author and poet**

For every fully grown, mature, and educated Southerner declaring, unequivocally, that Northern winters were never meant for human habitation, there's a Northern child staring through a frosted window begging his parents to let him stay home from school and tumble in that tantalizing white playground.

In fact, it could be argued that winters in the North were intended primarily for children. Few outside their world take such advantage of winter's possibilities. Even the most ardent cross-country skier, ice-fishing enthusiast, snowmobile fan, or skater can't compete with the rapture of a child's imagination when encountering a fresh snow-covered landscape. Only a playful god with a deep love of childhood could decide that this beautiful blue planet would be made more entertaining if seven inches of confetti were dumped upon it. No nearby swings, slides, or jungle gyms could ever offer as many options for a child's inventive mind.

Snow is a game changer. With a fresh covering, there is now more to do in the world of play than there are hours. Which is why children are so often overflowing with energy after a snowfall. Their wild creativity is fit to burst, and they can't get their boots, scarves, mittens, and coats on fast enough.

Imagine if you were a destitute carpenter, passionately in love with woodworking, but penniless. Then, overnight, the skies sent fine oak boards, saws, nails, and hammers to your backyard. You might ask, what have I done to deserve this? Children don't ask such questions, but construction equipment is also sent their way, free of charge. Everything they need to create their own home, fort, castle, or cave is right there. They don't require access to Mom or Dad's tool room; they don't need an older sibling's insights; they don't need to scour the alleys for old boards; they don't need to venture off to the woods for dead branches. Snow is construction equipment delivered with built-in screws and glue, with the only saws and hammers needed existing right there in the supple arms of every kid.

Snow can be anything one wants it to be. When I was a child, I would turn it into a tank and situate it on a nearby neighborhood intersection where cars crisscrossed. There I would have my pick of the enemy as they drove past. I could duck down inside my tank to avoid their fire, but they could do little to avoid mine. At night after supper, I could climb into my tank and wait for the car lights to come into view. I told myself the beams of light were their return fire, and my job was to avoid being hit by that light. When the beams did hit me, I was thrown from my tank, and sent tumbling down the snow-covered hill beside it. It was a fantastically dramatic death, and because I made the rules, it was but a temporary demise. There were more lives to live, more cars to take out, and more headlights to avoid.

I was cold and wet, but no matter. Snow was falling down my neck and onto my bare back, and every drip from my runny nose was freezing in place. Yet you couldn't have dragged me back home, not without parental threats. I was a tank commander, after all, a role I wouldn't have known one month earlier, when the frozen lawns were growing hard as concrete. Here, I could dive, I could leap, I could tumble, and in all directions protective drifts were there to keep me free from pain and tears. It was as if the gods had sent millions of fluffy pillows to our neighborhood. The winter air begged us to get outdoors and bask in the complete transformation of the rules of play. A new landscape was altering everything. The indoors was now but a prison.

Snow is wonderfully enticing to young children, but it is filled with devilish temptation for adolescent risktakers. One graduates from tanks and snow forts, sleds, and snowmen to thrills far more reckless. Sliding down a hill soon becomes sliding down a snowy garage roof out into the open air and down onto the piled-up mounds below. Innocent snowball fights in the backyard evolve into snowballs thrown at passing cars.

My friends and I did that far too often and deserved all the trouble we invited. When a young man with enough gumption would pull over to the curb and give chase, at full gallop, catching up to one or more of us and letting us know that this activity came with consequences, we took our punishment. But therein lay the thrill. Where was the fun in pelting the car of an elderly driver, when you could nail the windshield of the 20-year-old with the cigarette dangling from his lips? You knew he'd give chase, but you hoped he'd target one of your friends, instead of you, as you all scattered in different directions, hearing his deep voice behind you filled with vitriol and promises of retribution.

I would love to say that was the extent of our foolish risk-taking, but it continued to escalate from there. The most dangerous activity, and one I hope is no longer practiced by modern generations, was when my friends and I would creep up behind cars at stop signs and grab ahold of the bumper, or back quarter panel, so the drivers could give us free joyrides down the block, our boots sliding wildly across the icy streets at high speeds. In the darkness, the drivers were often oblivious to the those they were towing. It was exhilarating, and ridiculously dangerous, and our parents would have been horrified had they known. But we were kids, and we believed we could bend winter to our will. We were limited only by our imagination, and our imaginations knew no limits.

Picture having that much fun, on the Northland's finest natural playground, and then noticing the old well-to-do folks in the neighborhood packing up for their four-month escape to a Florida condo. It became, in our minds, the definitive act of growing old. The great surrender. It was the ultimate sign you were finished, your imagination dried up, the child in you withered away to nothing. You lived now for a soft chair and a TV remote. We reserved our deepest admiration for the aging neighbors, usually old women, who not only didn't leave, but wouldn't even let us shovel their walks for them. There they were, stringy gray hair protruding from ragged knit hats, huffing and puffing and hurling those heavy white flakes over their meaty shoulders. This was the image we thought should be front and center on any regional flag. They were our people. The snowbirds flying South were what we all swore we'd never become. We'd stay put until the day they dragged our wrinkled bodies kicking and screaming to a bed in a nursing home.

In our youthful minds, old age came when a person ceased believing winter was about opportunity, when one no longer saw that doors weren't closing due to the cold they were being flung open, in all directions. Rink rats knew all about this.

Every neighborhood of any decent size in the North has its share of "rink rats." This is not a pejorative but a term of endearment, meant for those who spend as much free time as possible each winter on the ice. They may play hockey for a local school or intramural league, but that's not nearly enough to satisfy them. They're found on the weekends and the evenings in the warming houses or out on the ice at local parks, joining pick-up games or firing pucks, solo, late into the night under the gleaming white lights that block out the black winter skies. From the street, passing by, you can see their breath moving out in short bursts, and hear the high-pitched scrape of their skates biting into the hard ice. Their graceful motions offer an extraordinarily beautiful alternative to the running so prevalent in most sports. Basketball, football, baseball, and soccer offer their share of graceful athleticism, but mastering that same movement on skates takes it to another level and brings the athlete closest to the sensation of flight. Watching a skilled hockey player move at high speeds, as if born with blades for feet, is akin to watching high-speed ballet.

I sometimes put together a fantasy scene, in my mind from long, long ago. Humankind is stumbling upon snow, ice, and cold for the very first time, having moved out of the savannas of Africa, migrating north. Eyeing the frozen expanse, some grizzled, weary traveler pulls out a long roll of tree bark and immediately begins listing all the new approaches to living that are going to be possible in this white world, all the different activities that can be pursued, the many ways they can take advantage of this new environment. The list grows long. It starts with sleds moving easily across the slick tundra and moves on to snow shelters and more playful images like snow sculptures and ice castles. It continues with the activities of ice skating, ice sailing, and ice fishing. A dozen people or more are now gathered around a large campfire, throwing out idea after idea, all inspired by the sudden appearance of this winter world. Then someone decides to wake the children and have them weigh in, and the list grows five times as long. And that lone roll of tree bark, held up for all to read, becomes the reason those weary travelers don't turn back and reclaim their former territory in Africa. Despite the hardships that will befall them in this bone-chilling new world, they've fallen in love with the idea of one season each year offering such an astounding shift in presentation, with so many new ways to experience being alive. Their world is given a kind of energy transfusion, a new and powerfully novel energy to keep the days on this earth from getting stale and boring. And the children are given the task of being the keepers of the scroll, reminding the adults why they stayed in this region. Every time some group leader complains about biting winds or the laborious act of shoveling, and suggests a return to their former homeland, the children are instructed to unfurl the scroll and take turns reading from the list until the group leader finally relents and calms down.

Children, of course, never need to be reminded of winter's glory. Adults do, and sometimes often. But isn't that the case in so many areas of life? We race from childhood as fast as we're able, only to spend our adult years longing for the delightful perspectives we had when we were young.

Winter is for the children, and falling back in love with winter, as an adult, means allowing the child still inside you to reemerge. It's a marvelous reunion.

Fire

"When the winter arrives, fire becomes a king."
— **Mehmet Muratildan, Turkish novelist and playwright**

There are no cultures on earth without deep appreciation for fire. Nowhere is a flame not seen as mysterious and enchanting. But, come wintertime in the North Country, those orange and yellow offerings that crackle, dance, and flicker attain a sacred status. We move beyond mere appreciation and place this lovely companion on a pedestal more often reserved for close kin.

Until you've sat by warming flames on a frigid winter night, you can't know fire's deepest blessing. Until you've witnessed the contrast of a roaring fire against a bleached white world of snow, you can't know its most angelic presentation. And I purposely use the word angelic because, as a Northlander, I'm annoyed when flames are used to represent hell and damnation. They should be held up as its opposite. They are often nothing shy of saviors, literally bringing succor to a landscape capable of draining the life out of all in its stinging grasp.

Flames are bewitching. Their presentation appears as a sophisticated form of art. They are mesmerizing, hypnotic, and playful. An Arabian proverb refers to fire as "winter's fruit." And the color of that fruit is dazzling perfection.

Some scientific studies have concluded that the most calming colors to humans tend to be in the blue family of hues. But that research must have been conducted in July. No one on a cold winter day in the North would deny that the orange and yellow of the flame present the most soothing, relaxing, inviting colors one could imagine. The sound of popping and crackling wood and the smell of fragrant pine can act like an opiate on the observer. A burning fire can hold one's attention for hours.

In fact, there's probably not a natural feature in a Northern winter that's ever been given the same degree of concentrated focus.

In Moby Dick, Herman Melville devotes a long passage to contemplating the allure of water. Whether a lake, stream, pool, or ocean, Melville wrote passionately of its mysterious magnetic pull and the way humans are endlessly found at a pier or shoreline, just staring at it. He wrote that there is "magic" in water and that "meditation and water are wedded forever." He believed we were beguiled because we were encountering the "image of the ungraspable phantom of life."

But Melville was born on the East Coast and spent his life on or near the ocean. Find me someone with Melville's insights in the land-locked North and my guess is the prose would shift. Northern writers might be in sync with Melville on a warm summer day, when the lakes and rivers are every bit as captivating as he described. But when that water freezes, it loses something. Not nearly as many people sit and stare with the same degree of wonder at a frozen lake. They look, but not as meditatively, not for prolonged periods. There's something that's gone dormant in that image. The life has been pulled from it. The energy, action, and magic are now over at that fire in that wood-burning stove, or fireplace, or the winter campsite. And those who might normally sit beside the waves, river rapids, or the shore of a placid pond, now prefer the flames. In fact, I could take Melville's writing and replace "water" with "fire," and make the same pitch to readers. Because everyone also knows meditation and fire are wedded forever, and that flames, too, are an "ungraspable phantom." And that all over the world men and women are drawn mysteriously, over and over again, to the flame, staring mesmerized, as if peering into infinity.

Clearing a Path

- a short story -

"Shoveling snow is my new meditation."
— **Mormei Zanke, Canadian writer**

Evelyn drove her shovel deep into the snow and checked to see if it had exposed the concrete sidewalk beneath. She wanted a clear, clean walkway this time. Her old shovel would always leave a thin, pasty layer of slippery white.

"There are two kinds of shovelers," her father used to say, "Those satisfied with a snowy path, and those who believe you keep a sidewalk as pristine as before the snow fell."

To accomplish the latter, she had required a new shovel, one with a sharper edge. It was the first new shovel she'd owned in six years, and it filled her with a buoyant confidence. The loud, biting scrape when the edge made contact with dry ground was deeply satisfying. It was the sound of a shovel doing its job, she thought. Any softer sound would have meant the blade was riding across a layer of snow, presenting a look that embarrassed her as a property owner. Her father had taught her better.

Evelyn's father had been an anthropologist. He had once told her that the very first shovels, going back to the Neolithic period, were made from the shoulder blades of oxen. He said the shoulder blade was known as the "scapula," and one could trace the roots of "spatula" and "spade" to that one word.

As she shoveled, she wondered what it would be like to be working with little more than a scapula right now. Momentarily, she wished for one, just to feel a connection to her ancient ancestors. Her father had instilled in her a passion for different eras and a desire to know a time she could never touch. Winter has a way of connecting people to the past, Evelyn told her children. Life got pared down to the essentials: Staying warm, staying dry, making a fire, making a meal, pulling on thick clothing, making it from point A to point B as best one could. A hot stew was a treat on a frigid afternoon, sure as it must have been a thousand years earlier. And the pain of cold fingers and toes was the same pain they felt in the Neolithic Period.

Winter made life tougher, Evelyn thought. And when life got tough, it came a step closer to the life of the Western pioneers. She occasionally asked her kids how they thought they'd stack up against the children of the frontier and privately wondered if she'd have been able to handle it as well. Where is that line where life brings too great of a percentage of pain without a sufficient percentage of pleasure? she wondered. She figured, if there were a place where her threshold of discomfort and misery might be met, it would be winter on the unforgiving plains in the 19th century. In her history books, she never read stories of suicide, but she figured many women must have considered it.

Evelyn went inside, after clearing the walkway, and poured herself a cup of coffee, then stared out the window from her wooden kitchen chair, feeling a kinship with everyone who had ever done the same, going back to the first winter shelters and the first sips of a warming drink.

"Life is just simpler in the winter," she said out loud, talking to no one. "Harder maybe, but simpler."

From the next room, her son David yelled, "What are you saying, Mom?" But Evelyn didn't hear him. She was noticing how the gusts of wind outside made the snow swirl above the drifts.

"Damn it, if that wind blows that snow back over the walkway, I'm going to be in one foul mood," she said.

"Mom, are you talking to me?" David yelled again.

She heard him this time.

"David, I want you to get my car off the street. The city's plowing today. Park it on Oak. But get it back out front this evening. Oak gets plowed tonight."

As she spoke, Evelyn heard her father's voice once again telling her how, before the Civil War, there were no snowplows. There were only snow rollers, giant wheels pulled by horses, compressing the snow to make it easier on the skis attached to carts and carriages. She wondered if the women back then might have preferred snow when traveling. Sure, it was a colder ride, she thought, but skis on compressed snow had to make for a far smoother trip than wooden wheels on rut-filled terrain. Winter took, she mused, but it also gave.

Her father had memories of traveling across the snow, pulled by horses. One memory was from Christmas Eve, 1927. He had lived on a farm as a child, in central Minnesota, just eight miles away from close relatives who owned a mercantile in the town of Little Falls. The relatives had closed the store early that December 24 to get ready for a festive Christmas Eve. Evelyn's father and his parents had been invited over for the night, which meant a one-hour, horse-drawn sleigh ride.

In the weeks since her father's passing, Evelyn often thought about that sleigh ride. To her, it was as idyllic a childhood memory as one could claim. She had asked him to tell the story on several occasions over the years, always in the winter, and most often at Christmas time, when his grandchildren were next to him.

That Christmas Eve in '27, her grandfather had heated bricks in a wood-burning stove. Then, using a small shovel, he'd placed the bricks on the flat wooden plank of the sleigh, each brick searing a rectangular char mark into the pine. He let the bricks cool until they wouldn't burn fabric, then placed quilts over them. Finally, he lifted Evelyn's father onto the quilts and piled more blankets over his son's bundled eight-year-old frame.

It was well below zero that night, and the winds were moaning. But Evelyn's father had told her he felt warm and comfortable. More than that, he felt an oscillating combination of exhilaration and serenity. He was with his beloved father and mother, and it was Christmas Eve, and what waited eight miles away was almost unimaginable joy. He was an only child, and the house he was heading toward would be filled with kids. That family was better off than Evelyn's father's family and they owned the mercantile, so they had access to wondrous gifts which were sure to be found piled high under the tree. The tree would be lit with candles, as was the German custom, and German carols would be sung. The songs would heighten the tension the children felt as they waited for the gifts to be opened. With each new song that tension would build until the wait would become unbearable. Anticipation could be delicious torture, Evelyn's father used to tell her, but it was torture just the same.

Evelyn's favorite part of her father's story was not the evening with his relatives, however. It was the sleigh ride itself and the way he spoke of it. He had recalled that the sleigh moved steadily and silently under a clear sky, and that at one point he had pulled the blankets down to the top of his lips, allowing the frigid air to sting him for a spell, just so he could take in the stars. He remembered not knowing what to make of the image above him. He recalled the peculiar way the stars seemed to draw him in yet frighten him at the same time. The night sky was a conundrum to a child, he had said. Beyond any kid's ability to make sense of it. It was where God lived, he'd been told, but God was impossible to comprehend as well.

Evelyn's father said that memory had stayed strong inside him all his life. He said there was something mysteriously soothing about hearing the threatening wind move through the tree branches above while feeling the protective warmth of the bricks below. In his child's mind, it was as if the wind were a woodland monster wishing him harm while the bricks were his parents' love, protecting him from all danger. He said it was, and remains, a perfect night, unlike any he would ever experience again.

Evelyn sipped her coffee and wondered if she had any childhood memories as sublime. She couldn't think of one. But she could bathe in the perfect memory of her father telling that story. The last time had been a month before his heart attack when her cousins, Gretchen and Will, were visiting from Georgia. They had never seen snow until that visit and were mesmerized by every view the town offered. They kept asking Evelyn if anyone ever died in the snow.

"Might someone fall and become buried beneath it, or might they get so cold they couldn't move and would freeze in place, alone, with no one to save them?" they had asked. Evelyn had laughed, thinking these were silly questions. "People don't die in the snow," she said. "Not in the city."

But a month later she would learn otherwise, when her father would collapse while shoveling. It would be just after supper, and he would be alone in the early evening darkness. No one would find him until morning. The paperboy would call it in. Evelyn was glad she'd not been there to discover him, hard as stone on that walkway, frozen brown eyes staring up into the empty sky, a sky she hoped his spirit had entered, joining the mysterious stars and the God he never did come to understand.

She would try to comfort herself in the days and weeks that followed by telling herself he had had a full life, and that she could keep him alive in her heart. But she soon came to view these as vacant words that did little more than keep the full weight of grief at bay. She ultimately rejected this approach and surrendered, allowing the fullness of sorrow and heartache to wash over her whenever it saw fit.

And it washed over her in the kitchen on this blustery morning with David in the other room watching TV. Thundering sobs, marching in slow moving waves of anguish, one after the another, forcing her to double over.

David came running into the kitchen, frightened. Awkwardly he held his mother.

"What is it, Mom? What's happened?"

When she didn't answer he asked again, before realizing it must be Grandpa. It had happened like this last month when he was visiting, and his sister said it had also happened when she was over recently. David told himself a whole year had to pass before this would finally stop. He didn't know where he had heard that, or if it were even true, but he preferred thinking of a set time in the future when he would not have to witness such pain. When his mother cried like this, she went someplace he'd never been, to a world he couldn't reach. He was removed, like a historian trying to touch some other era.

Evelyn felt the keening grief swirl inside her like black snow and felt the arms of her 24-year-old son trying to keep it from consuming her. Warmth and cold traded places, moment to moment; the cold of the icy silence, left behind by her father's passing, and the warm sensations of the love she felt from her son. There was a part of her that played the role of detached witness to the raw grief and the comforting blanket of David's arms, soothing as that warm quilt must have been to her father so long ago.

David had never been one for hugs, she thought, preferring to always come and go with a light kiss to her cheek. But here he was, tightly embracing her from behind, so that his head rested firmly against her back, his words repeating, "It's going to be all right, Mom. It's going to be all right."

The buffeting waves and the black snow slowly subsided. Evelyn's body relaxed, and she felt the full release of tension and stress. The calm after sobbing was a profound calm, she thought, deep and all encompassing. She told David she would be "fine now," that it was just her father's memory coming back again.

"It's nothing to get worried about," she said. "These things are going to happen. Someday, you'll feel the same for me. It's the natural way of things."

David offered her a glass of water, but she declined. She told him to go on back to what he was doing, that she was going to go outside again, to clear the snow that the wind had returned to the sidewalk.

"Oh, let it go," David said. "I'll take care of it later."

"No," Evelyn said. "You know how I like shoveling. And I need the fresh air right now."

Outside, Evelyn felt the winter move into her lungs and renew her, sending a crisp vigor through her aging body. She felt as if she'd just had a restful night's sleep. She lifted her face to the sky and felt massaged by the elements, the way a cool shower soothes on a hot summer afternoon. She opened the garage door and moved past her brand-new shovel to the back of the garage where an old shovel with a bent edge hung from a single nail on the wall. It was the shovel her father had been using when he died. She had brought it back to her place after the estate sale along with a few other items that didn't sell. She could never get herself to throw it out. It hung between a garden hose and a wooden step ladder.

She pulled it down and brought it out to the sidewalk. She took off her mittens, placed them in her jacket, and gripped the wooden handle with her bare hands, pushing the shovel slowly along the walkway. It gradually collected light flakes of snow, and she allowed them to build until the shovel reached the street, where she tossed them high into the swirling air. Some of the snow blew right back onto the walkway. Evelyn looked toward her house and saw that the shovel had left streaks of white all along the path, wisps of powder that had escaped the crooked blade. Some of it still moved, leaping up into the air with the blowing wind and coming down in a new spot, forming yet another swirl against the concrete.

She pulled up her collar, put her mittens back on, stared down the block in each direction, watching neighbors clearing paths from their front doors to the snow-covered street.

"It all comes back," she whispered. "It all comes back."

Jacket Johnny

"The sparrows are preparing for winter, each one dressed in a plain brown coat and singing a cheerful song."
— **Charles Kuralt, journalist**

Johnny took a quick glance at the online forecast for Aberdeen, South Dakota, but he ignored the featured illustrations, the image of a snowflake next to predictions of the day's accumulation or the swirly lines indicating brisk winds. Through his mind's eye, he saw only jackets.

In Johnny's perfect world, a different jacket would have been drawn for each variation in the forecast. And any radio weather reports would be delivered with thoughtful descriptions of the specific jacket required for that day. He then daydreamed that world into existence, grinning with his eyes closed.

"It's a real puffer-jacket day, folks," Johnny said, in his best radio voice. "And not just any puffer-jacket, one with down feathers from mature geese. There are too many immature duck down jackets circulating out there. Steer clear. And make sure your down has a fill-ratio of 550 or better. You don't want to skimp on a cold day like this. Tomorrow, we warm up to a simple, wool-lined corduroy, and it'll stay that way through the weekend. That is, unless your job has you working the graveyard shift outdoors, in which case grab a heavy shearling-lined hoodie and wear it under some waterproof polyester.

"The North is tailor-made for jacket junkies," Johnny told me, savoring the pun. He said he owned 18 currently and didn't view this as excessive. He said if he had the same number of shirts no one would bat an eye, and, in the North, "jackets are more important than shirts."

Johnny had separate jackets for temps in the 30s, temps in the teens, temps near zero, and temps far below zero. He also kept what he called a "stash late-autumn number" for the rare times 40 appeared on his winter thermometer. He had each of these jackets in three different fashions: what he termed "stepping out," "day-to-day," and "outdoor workwear." Some jackets were solely for wearing under other jackets. If visiting someone's lake cabin, for instance, the heavier jacket would come off, but the inner jacket remained because Johnny knew rural winter cabins were often cooler than city homes. He did the same thing at bars and restaurants, where the inside jacket came in handy when he was seated near the door. Some of those inside jackets appeared to be nothing more than light autumn jackets, but he insisted they were strictly winter jackets intended to be part of a cold weather ensemble. Of course, he dearly loved his many autumn jackets as well, and they also varied in material, color, and design.

Johnny talked incessantly and fervidly about his favorite subject, like a teenager describing a first love. His expressive baby face moved like a stage play below his blond crew cut. He could show incredulity, delight, and wonder all in a single breathless sentence.

Johnny told me he felt pity for those who lived where the climate was steady and a jacket arsenal unnecessary. "The jacket doldrums," he called these worlds.

He told me he relished the feel of jackets when first putting them on, the way they almost seemed to embrace him with compassion. If the jacket was vintage, he swore he could feel the years, all the seasons it had known, and the yeoman's effort it had taken to lend comfort. He said he cherished old photos of his ancestors in the jackets of yesteryear and marveled at how the styles had changed. All styles suited Johnny. None seemed out of fashion. Every jacket was a revered bridge between climate and comfort.

"It's the great equalizer," he said, slapping his hand on the table.

Dressing for winter was an avocation for Johnny, and when summer came, the sartorial monotony was a palpable letdown.

"Anyone can remove layers," he said. "The trick is in figuring out which layers to throw on in the first place and in what manner and in what style."

Johnny claimed dressing for a winter day could change his emotional state and his level of confidence. When he got it just right, he said the outdoors could feel like another room in the home, only more alive and vaster. It's then that he knew he had perfectly matched his ensemble with the weather. The comfort was exquisite, he told me, and the sense of satisfaction almost intoxicating.

He said he liked seeing what other people wore and in what manner they wore it and if they seemed comfortable or if they had mismanaged the whole process.

"Every winter you see the guys who dress for November in December or dress for December in January," Johnny said. "They're endlessly missing the mark, and you can tell just by looking at them. Their shoulders are up near their ears, and they're wincing. They're not happy. They botched it. They grabbed any old coat and gave the matter no more than a second's thought. Now they're uncomfortable, even in pain. And that makes them impatient with other people and irritable. But they've done this to themselves. I swear, I just want to tell them all to move to Barstow if this is the best they can do."

Johnny rarely uses the term "coat," because he doesn't appreciate what he calls "that weak single syllable." He is quite fond of the word "overcoat," however. He said there's a strength in that term, a gravity that matches the season. He is also fond of the term parka, though he uses that with only one of his closet offerings.

Johnny told me he knew that when he talked about all this with such passion, I could be put off and might view him as obsessive. But, he asked, would I say the same thing of an expert fly fisherman carefully choosing from an array of 60 flies, each having a separate story and separate purpose? No, he said. I would admire the dedication and expertise of that fisherman. "What's the difference?" Johnny asked.

Johnny opened a cedar chest and pulled out a heavy wool peacoat. He said two of his friends owned peacoats, but he didn't think they fully appreciated the design and utility of this Dutch invention.

"I really don't think people give a moment's thought to the miracle of wool. It actually adsorbs moisture. Not absorbs, adsorbs. How many even know that word?"

Johnny went on to breathlessly describe adsorption, where water molecules get trapped in the porous fibers of wool. Because the water is trapped, wool doesn't feel wet, even when it is.

"And the outer layer of wool actually gets rid of the water. It releases it back into the air as vapor. In fact, a certain type of wool, Merino, generates heat as it does this. It's like its own little furnace. It's astounding."

Johnny paused briefly, appearing concerned that he was coming off too strong or droning on, but then just as quickly plowed ahead, as if convinced only a fool could find this topic uninteresting. He pointed to the Ulster collar on his peacoat, named for the wet windy world of Northern Ireland. He said the collar was intended to button closed but would only do so with the eight-button peacoats, not the six.

"People typically wear six-button peacoats, never understanding how these things are supposed to work. If it doesn't have eight buttons, and by the way some rare ones have 10, then it's just a showy jacket made by someone who doesn't care about history. Six-button peacoats are now the most common. Can you believe that? That's what's happening to this world. We're losing our connection to the utility of things. There's a reason the British and American Navies adopted the peacoat. It's a marvel."

Johnny stopped to take a breath and appeared to ponder what more he wanted to say. I could tell he didn't want to stop, but he was 20 minutes late for work at a nearby bank. He started to bring up something called "the greatcoat," another wool creation that was much longer than the peacoat, but then stopped himself.

"There's so much more I could say. I wanted to talk about Eddie Bauer damn near dying of hypothermia back in 1936. It changed his life; did you know that? By 1940 he was receiving a patent on the down jacket. Do I like that Eddie suffered and almost died? No, but what a great moment in jacket history. And I haven't even gotten to my love for polar fleece, which wasn't invented until the 1970s. What a great decade that was for jackets, by the way."

Johnny was still talking as he threw on his wool duffel coat and walked out the door. He pulled up the oversized hood and struggled with the wooden toggle fasteners as he hurried to his car.

"You know anything about the duffel coat?" he shouted over his shoulder. "I have some more interesting jackets in the car that I'd like to show you, but perhaps a different time. I keep 'em there in the event that I stall out in a blizzard in some desolate environment and need to trudge out of there. They always say you're supposed to stay with your vehicle, but those people don't understand jackets. When you have a good jacket, you have a good friend. You're going to be fine."

Johnny opened his car door and turned to give me a hearty wave. He then slipped inside, revved his engine, and tore off down the road, revealing a license plate that read "BUT N UP."

Confessions
of a Weatherman

"Do you know what "meteorologist" means in English? ... It means liar."
— **Lewis Black, comedian**

I'm not going to give you my name. I don't want the baggage of what I'm about to say. Not because it isn't true. Because it's embarrassing. More than that, it could hurt my career.

I'm a TV meteorologist in a midsize market in the Northland. I hate the term "meteorologist," but that's what I'm called. A former college roommate of mine works at Harvard University and studies meteors. He's a global expert in the field. Is he called a meteorologist? Nope, weather guys stole the term. He's stuck being called a meteoriticist. He hates it, and I don't blame him, but there's nothing we can do about it now.

I used to work at a San Diego TV station, but I quit after one year. Weather in that town was an afterthought. No one was interested in talking about it. As the station's chief meteorologist, I was given less airtime than forecasters in any other American city. How many times can a person say, "Sunny and 75," before putting viewers to sleep? I burned up two years getting my master's degree in meteorology and another four getting my doctorate, all so I could say "Sunny and 75" five days a week. My co-workers viewed me as the butt of a joke. A San Diego meteorologist, they told me, was as necessary as sunscreen on a submarine.

I knew I could have gotten a decent job with the National Weather Service, but here's confession number one: I wanted to be a celebrity.

You'll never hear TV weather people say this, not so bluntly, but it's the truth. We want to be seen, admired, and recognized. We want to feel important. If you go to the website of the National Oceanic and Atmospheric Administration (NOAA) you can find an accurate forecast for your town. But those who worked to deliver it remain anonymous, and "anonymous" and "ego" are not compatible roommates.

Here's confession number two: I think I'm pretty good looking. I look at myself in the mirror and I feel like I won the lottery. My parents were both unattractive, but they must have counteracted each other's facial weaknesses, because the blend of their DNA produced something aesthetically pleasing. Even as a teenager, people talked about how handsome I was. I never wanted to waste that advantage. I figured if I added smarts to this face, I'd be in high demand in the TV world.

It worked.

I had several job offers right out of graduate school and opted for easy living in Southern California. But while I loved the San Diego lifestyle, I was horrified by how inconsequential I seemed. I came to the realization that if I wanted to be a weather superstar, I needed to go where weather forecasting truly mattered, where people talked about it all the time, in diners, in bars, at work, in the break room, on the bus. Wherever weather was king, that's where I wanted to be.

So, here I sit today, in the coldest part of the country, but with my face on a couple dozen billboards. I can't tell you what a high it is to not only be given a significant amount of airtime during my assigned evening weather slot, but to also lead the news occasionally, with severe weather warnings that could potentially save lives. It's not a stretch to say that, on some days, what I have to say is more important to viewers than anything else anyone will offer on that newscast.

I now have a real reason to get up each day. When it comes to weather, I'm the man. People respect me. They turn to me for insights. More than that, I often get the best table at local restaurants, with or without a reservation. The average schmo around these parts prattles on about the weather more than in any other region of the nation, and I'm their guru.

You can understand now why I need to remain anonymous. This is cringe-worthy stuff, were it attached to someone's identity. But it's refreshingly freeing in a world of anonymity.

On to confession number three. I have a morals clause in my contract. I am not allowed to be seen at a bar in this town. What I mean by that is the bar itself, not the restaurant the bar is in. Management doesn't want me seated on a stool in front of a bartender. That's where "drinkers" sit, they say. I can be seen nearby at some table, but not along the bar rail. I'd be okay with this except the same demands are not made of the sports anchors. Somewhere the notion was hatched that meteorologists seem more credible when they resemble Boy Scouts. Sports guys, on the other hand, are understood to be rough and tumble types who naturally enjoy a shot of whiskey and some barkeep banter. I've actually been told by our station consultant that I need to come across as if I "help old ladies cross the street in my spare time." He said a viral video of me so much as cussing could end my career.

I pass all this along as a way of helping you understand why it is that I occasionally drink, gamble, and carouse at all hours of the night when on vacation. It's something I need to get out of my system. There's a no-beard clause in my contract as well, so I never shave when I'm traveling. My wife accuses me of being some sort of "Jekyll and Hyde" type, but my therapist is far more sympathetic.

Here's yet another confession. I know that it's never going to be as bad as I'm making it sound when I deliver those distressing reports of an impending polar vortex or crippling blizzard. There are three reasons why I exaggerate consistently. First, it creates drama, and drama has appeal to most viewers. You like it, even if you claim you don't. The ratings prove it. Second, my role gets elevated in importance and appears critical to a person's daily commute or to parents getting their kids off to school. Lastly, it's just so satisfying talking this way. Admit it, going back to our days as children, all of us enjoyed stretching the truth or speaking in hyperbole to make our stories sound more impressive than they were. We meteorologists aren't immune to this. The cameras are on, the lights are bright, and we have the rapt attention of thousands. We're not about to tone it down. It's game on. This is showbiz, and we revel in it.

Finally, and here's where things are going to get a bit dark, a lot of you people out there are more messed up than we are. I deal with a lot of correspondence from viewers, and rarely is it enjoyable, engaging, or productive. It's mostly disturbing. A lot of you are way too into the weather. For me, it's my job. I get paid. You people obsess over it for free. I have no quarrel with someone taking an interest in weather, but the scathing emails I receive when I'm off an inch or two in my snow predictions or a degree or two in my temperature forecast, make me think it's more than an interest with many of you. Weather is your methamphetamine. And you're junkies.

Let's be clear, meteorology is an imperfect science. We're not going to nail it every time. Be happy we get close. Go back the span of one human lifetime, and there was no such thing as a highly trained meteorologist coming across the airwaves with helpful warnings and predictions.

The first televised weather report occurred in 1941, and it was delivered by a cartoon character named "Wooly Lamb." That was the level of gravitas to be found in your local forecasters. In the 1950s, the weather people were often forced to wear costumes and do stunts. Then came the weather-girl era: attractive young women without credentials passing along the next day's forecast with a pretty smile and nice hair. Now, when we have millions of dollars in modern technology and real science to go along with our hard-earned degrees, we're treated like we're "Wooly Lamb," modern cartoon characters flipping coins before each nightly forecast.

And it gets worse. In the forecasting community, we actually get blamed for much of the weather. If the winter is dragging on too long, we'll hear from many of you, in emails and angry voicemails.

"C'mon now, when the hell is it going to warm up around here? This is getting ridiculous. We shouldn't have to put up with this."

You think I'm joking? I'm not. Ask any seasoned meteorologist. They all have similar stories. We're seen as having some degree of control over outdoor conditions.

"This snow has become absolutely aggravating. Ten inches today after we just got done shoveling seven a week ago and six the week before that. What on earth is going on? This is nuts!"

I'll tell you what's going on. Weather. The kind that occurs in this climate. And know this, I'm not the one behind it. The manufacturing of low-pressure systems over Canada and the jet stream targeting of the northern U.S. are phenomena outside my skill set. Please understand, if I could control the weather, I'd be arranging a thick ice sheet for your driveway.

In the interest of full disclosure, I should pass along that I'm scribbling down all of this while sitting on a barstool in Chula Vista, 16 miles from my old Southern California stomping grounds. I've got a three-day beard and a three-drink buzz, and I'm taking this opportunity to get a few things off my chest. My wife encouraged me to put it down on paper so I could be done with it and we could enjoy some time together, without the background noise of my workplace musings. Of late she's been trying to get me to find the little boy inside me once again. The one who used to enjoy talking about weather because it was the spectacle of a planet in action, not because it made me feel important. When I was real young, the changing weather was the world telling me stories—soulful and emotive tales. The window was my movie screen. I was smitten. These days, I'm clearly more cynical.

But there still are those magical evenings when my world reaches a state of perfection, when I know something the general public doesn't, when I can stand before the green screen and talk of a town needing to shut down due to an encroaching winter storm, which will then be followed by record-breaking arctic air, sending the mercury plummeting to life-threatening lows. In that moment I feel a familiar fire in the belly and that tingling charge running through my spine. Suddenly, I'm like that kid who can't make it sound scary enough. I know you're all out there, maybe with your jaws hanging open, and I know you're going to be talking about everything I'm passing along—not just tonight, but for days to come. For the moment, in this town, I command the stage. The footlights are shining brightly, and I feel like this is where I was born to stand.

That might not be the little boy attitude my wife was hoping for, but that's as close as I get these days.

There you go. I've said it. I've dumped it all on paper. Now I'm ready to unwind and have a true vacation. Maybe the bartender will turn on the local news so I can laugh at my weather replacement at Channel 8. It's petty, I know, but it'll make me feel better about having abandoned these warm ocean breezes. Afterword, this Boy Scout plans to paint the town till the wee hours like a felon sprung from the hoosecow.

I sure hope my wife understands.

The Chilling

- a short story -

"Winter was a purifying engine that ran unhindered over city and country, alerting the stars to sparkle violently and shower their silver light into the arms of bare up-reaching trees. It was a mad and beautiful thing."
— **Mark Helprin, novelist**

A single chair was all he brought to this sweeping stretch of frozen lake; one wooden chair, in silhouette, against crystal white snow beneath a bold blue sky.

This is marvelous, Nick thought, as he gazed in different directions. A commanding blue dome, an expansive sheet of shimmering white, and one six-foot me, so meager by comparison, but pulsing with that same vitality.

The cold is a brisk balm, he determined. It can wake every sleeping cell in the body. It sharpens the mind and fires up the blood. Thoughts come into focus, clear and defined, and the sight of the breath gives one the sense of a body with its motor running.

Nick had not come here to fish, although from a distance that's what most would assume he was doing. He came because he envied ice fisherman. Not what they did, but the world they inhabited. They stood atop that deceptive foundation of barren ice, above a mysterious liquid universe of teeming life. Stretching out every which way was a vast milk-white desert, with the beaming sun above tucked into a boundless blue, making that sheet of white sparkle like a sequined gown.

Nick thought ice fishermen had the best seat in the house each winter, and though he never cared for the fishing itself, he loved being out on the ice, seated in his chair, taking in the vista. If he could change just one thing, it would be the questions. Passing fisherman always asked questions. The last one had prefaced his with advice.

"There's a sandbar just below you there," he had told Nick. "That may not be the best place to drill your hole."

"Oh, I'm not going to be making any holes," Nick had replied, smiling. A response that so often brought a long awkward pause.

"You're not going to make a hole?"

"Nope, I don't fish."

"What are ya up to then?"

"I just enjoy sitting here."

Nick knew that everyone continuing on after such an exchange viewed him as an oddity, somewhere between uncomfortably quirky and incomprehensibly eccentric. He had no pole or auger, but also no book, no magazine, no backpack, nor lunch bag. Just a single wooden chair.

Of course, when it came to eccentricity, those passersby didn't know the half of it. Three weeks earlier, the 62-year-old retired high school science teacher had brought his chair to the roof of his garage. There, he had pushed the legs deep into the snow, on either side of the roof's ridge. From that perch Nick had taken in his neighborhood with a tickling delight. He watched an old woman muscling snow from her sidewalk, a teenager cutting firewood by a toolshed, children skating with exaltation on a backyard rink, someone knocking icicles from above an entryway with a broom handle, a cat creeping along deep tire ruts in an alley, and a delivery truck struggling to make it up an icy incline.

Nick was entranced by this haphazard winter theater. The world appeared as an unfathomable chaotic mechanism with disparate, inexplicable moving parts randomly firing in all directions. He took it in, transfixed. Life appeared wholly fresh and novel from this perch. It was the first time he'd ever taken his chair that high, and he vowed to do it more often, despite the wary stares he received from below.

A woman who lived across the alley had pointed up at him while talking to her two young children. Nick knew it was doubtful that she was pointing out the whimsy of his roost and more likely that she was cautioning her children to keep their distance. Nick's reputation as a peculiar misfit was well-established in the neighborhood. While a few viewed him as a charming oddball, most were content to have as little contact with him as possible.

"We have to endlessly wake ourselves," Nick would tell his wife, when she'd grow weary of his offbeat pursuits. "It's our job as human beings. No one's going to do it for us."

"You go wake yourself," she'd retort. "The rest of us aren't sleeping."

Nick's wife had always made room for his unconventional passions, but she never wanted to accompany him on what he called his "Wake-Up Runs." She was reasonably content with him as a partner and viewed his unorthodox forays as a tolerable hobby, a harmless substitute for woodworking or golf.

Nick peered into the ice and snow below him, and then swung his head quickly into the rich blue above. He repeated this several times, giving his eyes a feast of nothing but white and then nothing but blue, over and over. As he continued, he laughed with light-headed wonder and noticed fresh thoughts springing forth: What a glorious combination, he told himself. These contrasting images of brilliant bright white and comforting deep blue, so alive, so absolutely alive. They carry a mysterious happy feeling, like kids at play. How different it will be tonight, Nick thought, when the white and blue vanish and stars come out against an eternal blackness. That's when this child's spirit will drift off to sleep and a shrouded grandfather will emerge for a long evening stroll.

He promised himself he'd come back after sunset.

On the shoreline, a bearded man in a thick, black snowmobile suit watched Nick through his binoculars. "What in the hell is he doing now?" he said, under his breath. He watched Nick's head swing skyward, straining, and then watched his chin come down swiftly almost to his chest, then back again.

"This guy's a piece of work," the man shouted, to his friend, who was busy adjusting the idle on a snowmobile 12 feet away.

"He was here the last two weekends," the friend replied, without turning around. "My wife gets a kick out of him."

"Well, I don't," the bearded man said, still staring through the binoculars. "He creeps me out."

"Why don't you go talk to him then," his friend said. "My wife thinks he's harmless. He doesn't bother nobody."

Nick stood up on the ice and looked off in the distance, then slowly turned his body 360 degrees. Where else around here could eyes see so far without interruption, he thought. How often in a day are eyes offered this much spatial freedom? He had recently learned that the edge of the earth as it curves away is three miles out. So, no one staring at any ocean is seeing more than three miles at a time. But looking up without obstruction, that all changes. Nick read that a communication satellite, spotted as a speck of light moving across the night sky, is 22,000 miles away and yet still visible. Most astonishing was that at night, one could see the Andromeda galaxy, a distance of 15 quintillion miles. Nick had slowly written out the number one afternoon. A 1 and a 5 followed by 18 zeros. He sat and stared at the number. He read that it would take 95 billion years to get there, using today's technology. And yet tonight he would enjoy it with a tilt of his head. With one slight upward turn, his eyes would carry him an ungraspable distance.

Thoughts like this could occupy and entertain Nick an entire afternoon. At times, he would just close his eyes, rest his head on the back of his chair, and listen intently, startled by the way sound traveled on a frozen lake and how easily he could pick up the casual conversations of fishermen far off in the distance. Or he would study a solitary black crow that had landed on the ice nearby. And he'd suddenly yearn to be a painter or photographer. A single, 20-inch black creature surrounded by a square mile of white powder was a scene begging to be preserved, he thought. The remarkable purity and simplicity of it left Nick engrossed and enchanted. This stark clarity was precisely what he longed for in his own life.

At first, the buzz of the snowmobile sounded more like a distant chain saw. As it grew louder, however, it drew Nick's attention. It was coming straight at him, a direct line from the shore. It was the bearded man.

From his snowmobile, the man could see Nick's gray hair being tossed by the breeze and, as he got closer, Nick's ruddy complexion.

Nick was in tan coveralls, wearing a fur parka with the hood down. The man drew close and confirmed there was indeed nothing out here but a chair. No fishing hole, no equipment. He drew alongside Nick and shut down his engine. Nick figured he was here to tell him about the sandbar.

"Can I ask what you're doing?" the man said, after removing his helmet.

Nick sensed agitation in the man's voice and replied with a smile, "Just enjoying the day."

"Just enjoying the day?" the man repeated, unsure where to go from there. He wiped small ice chips from his beard and his eyebrows. "Well, I tell ya, a lot of us who live on this lake are just wondering what your deal is."

Nick had not had an exchange like this before. He knew people viewed his behavior as mystifying, but he'd never sensed unease.

"I'm not here to upset anyone," Nick said, no longer smiling. "I just have an appreciation for this wonderful setting."

"Why don't you fish?"

"I'm not a fisherman."

The man looked down at the ground, as if unsure of what to make of such a statement. Then he found the words he'd wanted to deliver from the beginning.

"You make people a little uncomfortable, dude."

Nick turned his head and stared off in the distance, away from the man. He felt a growing tension gathering in his chest and a creeping sense of fear. He slowly rose to his feet and turned back toward the man.

"Is there any rule that says I can't be here?" Nick asked, his own voice revealing agitation for the first time. "I'm not on anyone's property."

"No, there's no rule," the man said. "I'm just trying to gauge what your story is. You've been here a couple of other times, and people are starting to wonder about you."

The wind blew puffs of white from the surface of the ice and they spun and twirled like small twisters. Crows dipped and darted overhead, dotting the blue sky like ink marks. But Nick looked at it all differently now. His light innocence faded. He felt nervous and self-conscious. No matter what happened in any further conversation, the afternoon seemed tainted. Nick sighed and slowly folded up his chair.

"I guess I'll be heading out," he said.

"Well, that's up to you," the man replied, his tone now softening. "But I felt within my rights to get a handle on things. You can understand that, I'm sure."

Nick didn't say anything. He tucked his chair under his arm and walked in the opposite direction from where the man had come, expecting to soon hear the snowmobile engine start. But it didn't. So, Nick figured his exit was being studied. As he listened to the crunch of his boots against the snow-covered ice, he thought about the stare he couldn't see. Was it a stare like the mother's back home, he wondered. Was it the stare her children would one day adopt? The thought depressed him. So, he chose, instead, to change his vantage point.

Fifteen quintillion miles away sat the Andromeda galaxy. He had recently read that it's speeding our way at a quarter of a million miles an hour, and that in four billion years it will collide with our Milky Way, creating an incomprehensible spectacle in the sky. No one will be here to view it, of course. By then the sun will have boiled away all the lakes and oceans. But Nick's imagination was stationed there right now, taking it in with awe.

Suddenly, all was wonder once more. Like a fish thrown back in the water, Nick slipped back into his natural state. He climbed the steep bank to his waiting automobile, invigorated by the spectacle of an impenetrable and bewildering universe.

Sport in Winter

"They who sing through the summer must dance in the winter."
— **Italian proverb**

My name is Karla Delzean. I ride a motorcycle in the summer and a snowmobile in the winter. I also water-ski in the summer and snow-ski in the winter. And some friends and I enjoy playground basketball in the summer, and those same friends join me for pond hockey in the winter. If given a choice, I'd prefer the weather that accompanies my summer activities. But, without exception, I receive more of a thrill from my winter pursuits. They offer more pleasure and gratification than their summer counterparts. And this is the reason I don't move back to South Carolina, where I grew up. I have fallen for pastimes available only in the world of snow and ice.

It's no easy thing explaining to my Southern kin the intoxicating sensation of riding a snowmobile through a narrow wooded trail and out into an open field that's covered in thick, soft powder. I tell them of sailing across that tremendous expanse all alone, the first one to do so, following a great snowfall, zigging and zagging at will beneath the bluest of blue skies, and sensing an earth below made of the lightest and most supple of substances, creating the notion that I have shifted to riding across a passing cloud. It's just me, the cloud, and the serene blue sky, and the speed of my machine fills my body with adrenaline. When I conclude that ride and shut down the engine, taking in that strange quiet that is wintertime in the countryside, I feel as though the season and I have just meshed, fully, and I feel married to every sensation, every vista, every white flake covering my clothing.

But, when I gauge their reaction, I'm aware I'm not doing justice to the experience. Descriptive sentences can't recreate an experience that careens through the five senses and calls on the deepest of emotions. Words only paint around it. In the center of that experience there are no words.

I love my motorcycle. But when I'm riding it, I can't arrive at comparable sensations, even along a beautiful country road on a colorful autumn afternoon. I can get close, but that's it. I'm too grounded, too walled in by familiarity and structure. Winter, consequently, will always be a part of my life.

I could make similar arguments about skating, how there is something unearthly about competing in a sport where everyone has agreed to find something akin to a sheet of glass on which to move, and to do so with thin blades that will take everyone to speeds they could never attain in any other team sport utilizing two legs. But, with skating, I hope all I have to do is place in someone's mind the image of going backward at those speeds. This is the moment when hockey becomes something truly remarkable. It's in that moment when I turn around and feel myself moving just as fluidly and swiftly backward, that I never fail to experience the key difference this sport offers and how exceptional it is as an activity. No soccer or basketball player, running backward, can ever know such flowing graceful mobility.

As for the snow-skiing and water-skiing comparison, there's no contest here. In one, you're tethered to a boat. Your hands are slaves to a rope. The water is refreshing and delightful, but unmitigated freedom is absent from the adventure. With snow-skiing you make choices with every moment on the slopes, where to go and how fast to do so. Gravity takes all stress from the endeavor. It's freefall, but with agency.

If I look for the common denominator in these winter hobbies, I find it's the way the frigid season shifts the commonly experienced laws of earthly physics. It takes the body to places it cannot know on a planet called "Spring Summer and Fall." It whisks a person away to some far-away world where everything is topsy-turvy for a few months, before setting them back down again in April and opening the gates to the familiar world of grass, dirt, and asphalt.

Winter offers a strange, whimsical otherworld, but a comparative few choose to know it, in the deepest, fullest sense. It holds out its hand but doesn't beg us to come along. Those who choose to, however, never view the season the same way again. They become part of a congregation who knows its own peculiar version of enlightenment. It's a seasonal enlightenment. It's an awakening to another part of you that can come out to play in a whole new way. Of course, it's not for everyone; perhaps not even for most. But that just makes it all the more endearing to me.

I was raised in Charleston, amidst the heat and those born to it. The North has fiercely ushered in my rebirth. I'm a winter girl now. There's no going back.

Push

> *"Winter is not a season, it's an occupation."*
> — **Sinclair Lewis, novelist**

"Roll down your window... Keep it down so you can hear me... Now, put your car in drive, but don't give it any gas just yet... Put it in drive and keep your foot on the break... Got it?... Now, wait till I say go and then give it gas, but when it moves forward, let up on the gas and let the car roll back again, then give it more gas till it moves a bit more forward, then let up. We're going to get your car rocking, back and forth, okay? ... So, give it gas 'til it moves forward, then let up till it moves backward, then repeat, over and over. We need some momentum here... Okay, ready, go!... Yeah, that's good, that's good... Now let up... Now give it gas again... Good... Now let up... Keep doing that... Yes, yes, yes... Keep it up... That's it... Keep it up, keep it up... You got it... Okay now just gas, just gas, just gas... Go go go... Yes, yes, yes you got it! You're out! You're out!"

What year did words like these first accompany the visible steam moving in staccato bursts from the mouths of bundled Northerners, straining on some snow-covered roadway? On what blustery winter day was such chatter first aimed at a driver in a bind? Decade after decade, it's been the same advice, given by someone staring with grim determination at tires spinning in place.

"Push, everyone, push." A shout heard above the roar of a revving engine. Three, four, five people, bodies bent against the rear bumper, boots dug into a white mound, shoulders pressed against cold metal, voices groaning. "Puuuuush...!"

The first time you try to push a car through the snow with human muscle it's a rite of passage. By the 30th time it's a well-rehearsed play. But over the years it becomes a sacred, beautifully choreographed ritual. Finally, late in life, such acts are engaged in as therapy, as necessary to the soul of a Northerner, so as to continue to tightly knit that intimate connection to the season and to provide a sense of place. Ultimately, it serves the helper with the muscle far more than the driver with the problem. Pushing a vehicle out of the snow is a Northerner's touchstone. It helps solidify our identity the way a uniform might for a Boy or Girl Scout. The Scouts have merit badges that move them gradually along to some higher plane. Northerners have rituals that move us deeper into who we are.

The guy on the corner starts his snowblower and clears his walkway. As he nears his property line he pauses, and then decides not to turn around. Instead, he keeps moving in a straight line past the next house, and the next, and the next. What's he doing? You spot the heads in nearby windows as neighbors peer out.

"There goes Roger," someone says. "He's going to tackle the entire block. He's cutting a swath for everybody."

Why is Roger doing this? First and foremost, Roger knows that only a few neighbors have a snowblower, and he feels stubborn pangs of guilt when he's seen clearing his walkway effortlessly while they grimace with a shovel. Secondly, Roger longs to be a good man. He doesn't find as many opportunities as he'd like, but here's one. Everyone in the neighborhood on this day, will see that Roger can be a decent guy. Sure, he drinks too much and he's a blowhard and his car could use a muffler. But there's a good heart in there. That's what Sara is going to say, in a minute or so. She's going to turn away from her window, walk past her husband, and say, "That Roger's okay."

In the wintertime you need to be okay. You can be a jerk come summer, but winter is when you need to be better. It's when you need to look out for other people. Old people fall, homeless people shiver, cars smash into one another, people find themselves alone for the holidays. A Northerner needs to be aware, needs to be conscious of his or her surroundings, needs to move through the day with an understanding of community. It's how Northerners have gotten by since people first moved to this region. It's not about selflessness. It's about how we all make it through. It's how life is made easier, for everyone. And, as with the person pushing the car free of the snowbank, the beneficiary is almost always the one providing the aid. In that service you become more of who you're meant to be, and you embrace that. You feel yourself slip into that comfortable sense of being a decent person, and it feels as warm as a favorite sweater. A familiar light enters you. It's a communal light, one that bonds you to the group, that makes where you live something more than a location on a map.

We push, we Northerners, we push. Along with the cars and snowblowers, we push ourselves to be compassionate. It doesn't always come naturally, which is why the season is a gift. And the season pushes us in return. Some are pushed right out of the region, down to the sunny South. But those who remain have a way to make it through. No matter how cold the temps get, those temps are no match for the warmth of human empathy.

Andrew is pushing a shopping cart filled with blankets, clothes, and plastic shopping bags containing toiletries and canned goods. He's on his way past the park and across the busy street to some nearby railroad property. Before the tracks appear, there's a clustering of trees and a meager pond. Tucked beside the thick exposed roots of a massive oak tree there's a blue tarp weighted down with rocks and tied in place with twine. This is home. Andrew has a propane stove but no propane. The tank is empty. He'll have to head to that well-traveled intersection a mile away to stand with his cardboard sign and his 15-gallon propane tank. The sign is specific. "Just want to be warm. Please help." The heater is not used for warmth as much as it is for cooking, but Andrew wants a sign that will keep it simple.

Few people can argue with the way a tattered fellow with a cardboard sign can appear more in need on a cold January evening than on an August afternoon, even with the general presentation of that person being roughly the same. As one pulls up to an intersection, the situation seems far less like desperate desire and far more like emergency need. Cold changes everything. First, it takes far more gumption to stand there, shivering, asking for money. And for the person driving by, just the idea of being homeless in such weather is disruptive to the heart. Dollars pass through the rolled-down window with more frequency. The contrast between the person with the sign and the driver in his or her warm car goads the conscience more dramatically than a few months ago.

The internal and external forces that push each of us in winter include the push we all receive to get outside. It's sometimes battled by the pull of one's dwelling, the pull of one's couch, the pull of a book or film, and the pull of comfort food and blankets. But unless you absolutely can't handle what's on the other side of those walls, there is that push to routinely breathe fresh air and move your body, and that means the push to leave that snug world with the thermostat set at sweet 70. There are three ways Northerners receive the push: grudgingly thoughtfully, or enthusiastically.

Grudgingly means a quick walk around the block, maybe a bit farther in mild temps, but not a whole lot farther. You're not doing this for enjoyment. And grudgingly means only the basics: gloves, hat, coat, and boots, that's it. The walk is swift and is intended to assuage the nagging guilt that you might be harming your health with your sedentary winter ways.

Thoughtfully can mean a simple walk as well. But it's long and it's planned and it's with the realization that, no matter how cold it is, there's clothing to keep you comfortable. A base layer to wick away moisture and insulate, a light, flexible mid-layer to trap body heat, and a tough windproof outer layer with a good hood. Long thermal underwear and loose-fitting moleskin pants work together to trap heat, and you're pushed to move at a healthy clip because movement adds warmth. The time outdoors can be invigorating, and it makes your return home all the more rewarding. On a star-lit winter night, after a good snowfall, where you're the only one outside in that deep quiet, it can be a sacred service to your soul, not just a boost to your cardiovascular system.

Some people are pushed to go further in their outdoor pursuits and become winter sports enthusiasts. They're pushed to learn to skate or ski, or they buy snowshoes or learn to ice fish, or they make sure they get out tobogganing with their kids on the weekends. Surrounding Northerners in all directions are winter's unique opportunities. The necessary incentive to explore those opportunities can be nothing more than the often-repeated warning of our elderly citizens:

"What you will come to regret most at the end of your lives," they tell us, "are not those things you tried and failed at or that you found wanting. It will be all those things you never tried at all."

Winter pushes Northerners to reflect. The cold and dark make it almost impossible to avoid taking time to look deeply into one's own life. We are all pushed inward, and in so doing we're pushed to evolve. And there is little deep reflection in a human life that isn't followed by some desire for change. Winter is often the gestation period for change, with spring presenting the perfect setting for its birth. In this way winter is deceptive. All is quiet, frozen, and still. But it's the season best suited to kick-starting our most dramatic transformations.

We just need a little push.

Envy

- a short story -

"The hard soil and four months of snow make the inhabitants of the northern temperate zone wiser and abler than his fellow who enjoys the fixed smile of the tropics."
— **Ralph Waldo Emerson**

Todd viewed the graceful palm tree towering over the gray-white sand and the green-blue ocean. As he felt the sun on his neck and the cool of his mojito in his hand, he knew it wasn't enough to privately own this moment. He needed to let someone else know he was enjoying it and, just as importantly, that they weren't.

So, he texted his brother Eric in Fond du Lac, Wisconsin, where the temps were in the teens and the skies were bland as bankers' slacks. It was his third text to Eric that week, always with the same theme.

"Life's pretty good here, Bro," he typed. "Probably as good as it gets. Cheers from Miami."

Eric received the text as he pulled into his driveway. He heard the familiar notification on his cell phone and looked to see who was contacting him. With his car idling and the heater blowing softly, he stared at the image from Florida. He considered texting a lone thumbs up. But he'd done that the last two times. So, he went in a different direction.

"What is it about people who leave Wisconsin for a tropical vacation?" he typed. "They can't enjoy themselves, not fully, not completely, until they have let someone else back home know how much better their situation is than that of the poor schlub stuck on the tundra. What part of your psyche is fed by this practice? Why is it necessary, in order to enjoy your day on the beach, to let someone who's not on the beach become aware that you're on the beach? How unfortunate that a good day isn't truly good, until someone else, who's not enjoying it, knows about it."

Todd received the text and read it twice. He couldn't tell if Eric was being facetious. He often had this problem with his brother's messages. He couldn't get a sense of the tone. Was Eric truly annoyed or just teasing? Todd determined that the words hit a little too close to home. In fact, they stung. Eric is being sincere, he thought. He had hoped Eric would type, "You lucky bastard." But it was true, Todd couldn't quite feel like a lucky bastard until someone who wasn't a lucky bastard called him one. He suddenly felt exposed. He typed back, "You're just jealous," words he longed to be true.

Eric typed his reply quickly. "Jealous? Thus far your thoughts are not with your surroundings but with making sure others are aware of those surroundings. That doesn't come across as an enviable state of mind. The photo you sent shows a landscape but not a state of joy or an experience of pleasure. What conversations are you having and with whom, and how rewarding are they? Is the time away helping with your insomnia? I just learned from Nancy that your boss is being transferred to hospice care. This can't be the best time to be away from the office. Is any of this occupying your mind as you feel the warmth of the sun on your 51-year-old body? Call me when you get back in town and we'll go out for a scotch and talk about it. Maybe the window seat at Schiller's. We'll watch snow fall and listen to those Nat King Cole Christmas carols on their juke. Meanwhile, here's a photo of my car, idling in the driveway. I'm staring at the cold ground, captivated by the dance of the exhaust above the icy concrete... Safe travels, Brother."

Todd put his phone down, agitated by the exchange. No more texts to Eric, he thought. He considered texting the beach scene to someone else, someone less prickly. Maybe Steve, his assistant. Then Todd realized how little weight Steve's reply would carry. He needed acknowledgment from a peer.

He scrolled though his contact list. He couldn't find anyone he judged as having sufficient gravitas. Except for his boss. So, against his better judgment he clicked on her phone number and copied and pasted the photo of his idyllic beach scene. He spent a couple minutes trying to decide what words would be appropriate, given her situation. "Life doesn't get any better," was no longer an option. He chose instead what he thought would be a compassionate message. He typed, "I'm praying this is what the afterlife looks like," and pressed send.

Within seconds, he regretted it. Overwhelmingly. He felt a dense rush of remorse move across his chest, followed by a far deeper and burdensome shame. It sapped all the thrill from his vista and all comfort from the ocean breeze. Guilt-ridden and beside himself, he set down his Mojito, gripped his forehead and said, in a whispered grimace, "Shit, shit, shit."

Back in Wisconsin, Eric had walked next door to offer aid to his neighbor, who was clearing snow from his rooftop. They had chatted briefly, and Eric was now holding the man's ladder in place, while keeping his head down to avoid the cascade of cold powder being sent from above. Then Eric heard, once again, the familiar high-pitched tone of yet another text notification coming from inside his breast pocket. He removed his glove, pulled out the phone, and saw that it was Todd, passing along in capital letters that he had just received an angry text from his boss's husband, and did Eric have time to talk.

Eric sent a selfie as a reply, showing snow covering his hair, eyeglasses, and beard. He typed, "No. But wish you were here."

The reply from Todd was immediate: "Me too."

God & Winter

"How many lessons of faith and beauty we should lose if there were no winter in our year."
— **Thomas Wentworth Higginson, Unitarian Minister**

Our seasonal visitor is often referred to as "Old Man Winter," and I used to ponder that moniker. Why "old man?" Because he's wise? Because he's tired and worn out? Because aging hair can turn white as snow? I eventually learned we can pin it on the ancient Greeks. They believed a very specific god ruled over the north wind. That god, Boreas, was always depicted as an old man, with a short temper and a prickly disposition. They claimed he brought the cold, and that the severity of each winter season depended on his mood that year.

But the Ojibwa tribe of Northern Minnesota also saw winter as an old man. They called him Peboan and said he would walk across the land and, wherever he stepped, the Earth would turn "hard as flint." His long locks of white hair would drag behind him, covering everything. Birds flew and animals hid from his cold gaze. They said his icy breath made the streams stand still.

An old and ornery man, that's who was blamed for winter. How different would our current perspectives be had a fair young maiden been handed that responsibility; an angelic beauty who draped the dry brown tundra in her flowing white gown and took her thick dark hair and created the long sacred nights so we might sleep peacefully, enveloped in her flowing locks? "Young Woman Winter," I think I'd have preferred that.

"Old Man Winter" makes more sense if one thinks strictly in terms of the stages of life. If spring is when we're born, summer when we flourish, fall when we age gracefully, and winter when we die, the old man label is fitting. And in that image of winter, it's understandable why it would be seen as a season for going inward. Not just going indoors, but going inside ourselves, to reflect on our lives, looking for meaning in the arc of our existence.

It's no surprise that the second half of life tends to be the time when people look beyond relationships, children, and career, and earnestly contemplate the existential questions. What's it all about? Is there something more I should be grasping, something I could learn, were I to slow down, rid myself of frivolous distractions, and spend time in meaningful reflection? The final years of a human life can provide ample opportunity for this. But so can the season of winter, all by itself. It's a season ideal for spiritual reflection.

We get our cue from nature. Many insects go into a state of suspended animation in the cold season. "Diapause" it's called. All their busy activity slows until finally there is no movement whatsoever. Some of them are literally frozen in place yet still alive. The warm spring will bring their miraculous rebirth, but now is the time for stillness. And "stillness" is the word most commonly employed by the great religious traditions when describing the necessary conditions for communion with the source of creation.

Regardless of one's spiritual beliefs, I believe there's no denying that who we truly are is not to be found in the chaotic thoughts, sensations, emotions, and perceptions of the body and mind. The very fact that we can each observe those thoughts, sensations, emotions, and perceptions tells us there is something resting outside of them, something we're rarely able to get in touch with in the frenzy of our busy lives. Winter gives us opportunity, however. In all manner of ways, we are being called to shift. It isn't just the insects slowing down. All plant life is going dormant. The abundant and colorful foliage that was there just months earlier has faded to something still and muted. We are part of that natural world. What shift are we making?

With the sunlight fading, the land appearing barren, and the piercing cold seeming so inhospitable, the great spiritual traditions of the world chose this very time to hold some of their most sacred festivals and to fashion their most powerful myths. They too saw dormancy and darkness as an opportunity. Born were the ancient winter solstice myths that, in their various manifestations, have a lingering hold on much of humanity to this day.

When one witnesses a bountiful, flourishing world of color and teeming life reduced to a cold, stark, austere landscape, the metaphor of our own death is inescapable. It is a reminder that ultimately everything we love and cherish will be taken from us, some of it while we're living, the rest when we ourselves pass. It is sometimes astounding that we don't all grow depressed by this reality. Yet most don't. In fact, many live lives of great contentment. Paradoxically, in many surveys the elderly report levels of happiness far surpassing that of younger people. In their own season of death, they live with their greatest joy.

There is a way in which winter teaches us to put death in a fresh perspective. There is a profound difference between thinking of death as a point at the end of a linear journey, versus a point on a circle. Winter is a stage in a repeating cycle. Come the end of December, with the darkness dominating the day, new light is born, which will grow steadily the rest of the winter and throughout the spring. This is as hopeful a thing to witness in nature as there is. And if we are part of it all, might this be our story as well?

Long nights and darkness are often associated with the subconscious, with dreams, and with the spirit realms. In this way there is something naturally mystical about winter. All the great religions traditions have viewed the season as presenting spiritual opportunity in one form or another.

The Rabbi Judah Loew ben Bezalel lived in the 1500s in Prague, in what is now Czechoslovakia. He was a Jewish scholar, philosopher, and mystic who promoted the idea that winter occurred outside of time. The dormancy seen in the natural world was a dormancy in all things, he said. He believed that stillness was a sign that we were no longer living in the world of time, where action, growth, and movement were found. It's an extraordinary thing to contemplate moving into a season that's outside of time. How does one approach life in that context?

Rabbi Boruch Leff, an author and a speaker on topics of Jewish spiritual life, says, "The Jewish bible did not give us any winter holidays (Hanukkah is one of the least significant and was not mentioned in the Jewish bible). There must be a reason for this. It must be that it is not the time for making great spiritual leaps, but rather a time to reflect on what we have already gained, spiritually." According to Rabbi Leff, winter offers an opportunity to slow down and not reach for more to add to one's spiritual plate or put pressure on oneself to advance. But instead to pause, settle in, and reflect.

And one of the things Rabbi Leff likes to reflect on is snow. He has written eloquently of its sacredness. He cites an old Jewish teaching describing the land of the earth as having been made by the snow that rests under God's throne.

"This alone speaks of the close relationship of snow to God," Rabbi Leff says. The idea that it sits beneath His throne should remind the world of its sacredness. Snow reminds us that God, who is sending it from the heavens, is the reflector of all wisdom. Contemplating snow's profound meaning helps us feel connected to Him."

Adherents of Islam often quote the prophet Muhammad as saying, "Winter is the best season for the believer." Ramadan, the most sacred month of the year for Muslims, can come in any season since Muslims follow a lunar calendar. The devout abstain from food and drink during the daylight hours of Ramadan, so when that holy month comes in the winter Muslims have it easier.

Umar bin al-Khattab, one of the most influential Muslim caliphs in history, said, "Winter is the prize of the worshipers."

The Muslim scholar Ibn Rajab said, "Winter is the best season for the believer because Allah strengthens his practice by making worship easy. In winter, the believer can fast during the day with ease and without suffering from hunger and thirst. The days are short and cold, and he therefore doesn't feel the hardship of fasting. And due to winter's long nights, one can have his share of sound slumber and still have time to wake before sunrise for the necessary predawn prayers. Thereby it becomes possible to fulfill the interests of both his religion and the comfort of his body."

Native American tribes in the Northern United States saw the world go dormant in winter, and they too viewed it as a metaphor for going inward. Winter provided them with fertile darkness and long silence, out of which new inspiration could emerge. And it was always story-telling time. Traditional tales were often reserved for the cold months when it was said "time slowed down." The busyness of growing, gathering, and hunting food in the spring, summer, and fall was replaced with long nights, seated around a warming fire, passing along ancient tales. Many of the stories featured animal characters, and certain tribes would say they waited until the winter, when animals were hibernating or less active, so the creatures couldn't hear themselves being talked about.

Many Christians also embrace the spiritual opportunities winter provides. Matthew Fretwell, a Christian theology professor, wrote that as sure as a gardener understands that a good freeze in winter prevents certain insect gestations and promotes soil stabilization, the ceasing of frenzied activity and turning toward deep, quiet reflection can serve the soil of the soul.

"Jesus explained times of 'pruning' for believers," Fretwell wrote. "He expressed that the same laws we see in nature apply to the spiritual. To be fruitful means there must be times of cutting back. Winter is necessary to manifest the beauty of spring—renewal and rejuvenation. Likewise, the Christian life needs pruning back. The winter seasons of life prepare us for the growing season. Our times of cocooning will bring about a butterfly-type spiritual transformation. Don't neglect the winter seasons of life as unfruitful. Think of them as times of preparedness. Winter is necessary."

Christopher Asmus, a Christian pastor, wrote, "When it snows, some Christians become functional deists. Deists believe God created all things (like weather) and then stepped back to passively let creation (like snowstorms) run its natural course. In other words, we see snow as an interruptive act of nature, not an intentional act of God, and so we grumble. But God's fingerprints are on every flake. Every flake is sent to show his splendor in snow, his beauty in a blizzard. When we see banks of snow piling up, we should say, 'It's just like his grace—abundant and heaping.' When we look outside and see only winter white, we should say, 'Preach, snow!' "

Hillary Nicholls is an energy healer. She believes that some people turn away from winter because, in the darkness and quiet of the season, they often feel the discomfort of emotions they didn't take time to look at and process in the spring, summer, and fall.

She wrote, "If we don't allow ourselves to see and feel the darkness we carry within, we can project those feelings onto winter itself and blame the season for bringing us down when it's actually something calling out to us from deep inside."

Many Buddhists will say darkness, when it's all around us, invites us to look for the light inside us, the most important light of all. And it is often in the dark, cold months that we are gently but continually prodded to search in earnest for that inner light, to find something that is unperturbed by changing seasons. Ultimately, many Buddhists will say, we don't truly chase away darkness by stringing holiday lights, but by finding the eternal light we all carry. In this way, winter is a great spiritual gift and teaches us once more that only in having experienced darkness can we ever know light. Only in contrast does light makes itself known.

Theresa Scherf lives a hermetic existence in a two-room log cabin in Northeastern Montana. She said she moved there to spend the last third of her life "finding a deeper connection to the mystery of life." She said a snowfall is the one thing that never fails to place her in a "state of grace," and she's come to view it as nature's most sacred act.

"I always feel indebted to snow. The sight of something so pure and so angelic falling from the heavens immediately arrests my attention and I stop what I'm doing to feel a great calm come over me.

"Notice what a snowfall actually does. It demonstrably stills the world. It covers plants and those things that otherwise might move with the wind. As it falls, things settle in place, and the world gets noticeably quieter. Snowfall has the power, all by itself, to immediately shift one to a state of contemplation. The world after a snowfall appears hushed. I don't know any individual act of nature that speaks more directly to the soul, that sends such a strong message, and one we all need to hear."

The Reverend Josh Pawelek, a Unitarian minister, believes winter carries us away from physical reality and into mystical realms.

"I imagine winter as the womb season," Pawelek wrote. "A floating, sleeping, dreaming season, one for gestation, for growth beneath the surface, in the nurturing darkness. I imagine winter as the season for preparation, for getting ready—ready for new selves."

Winter has the unique ability, overnight, to place one in a state of awe. In a matter of just a few hours, the world can appear utterly transformed. Standing at the window and experiencing awe, one touches the sensation most associated with the deepest spiritual insights and awakenings. When encountering the divine, awe is a richer and more fitting human expression than words are capable of conveying. Awe is that sensation of being in the presence of something infinitely greater than oneself. So, my favorite experience in the winter is that feeling of awe. It's when I'm at the limits of my ability to know, and when I must then surrender, and allow myself to fall into the waiting arms of that great and holy unknowing, in all its ineffable grandeur.

Winter Window #2

Isabelle rests against the window
holding her steaming coffee with both hands
Her eyes scan the backyard
like a finch seeking a perch
In the moody twilight
her gaze comes to rest upon the lonesome stones
of an idle fire pit
near forlorn patio chairs

She remembers a last autumn gathering with friends
Flashes of plaid, smoke, and laughter upend the bleakness
She whispers, "This is the grave where memories lie"

An arctic breeze begins a ghostly dance with a tire swing
Now, her grandson's unruly hair and spindly limbs
command the slideshow of her memory
He's twirling, dizzily
layers of foliage spinning past him
a kaleidoscope blur

The laughter fades
She watches the empty swing move hauntingly
in a world without leaves
without flowers
"My yard is a crypt," she says
and draws the blinds

Skating in the Dark

- a short story -

"Into the darkness they go, the wise and the lovely."
— **Edna St. Vincent Millay, poet and playwright**

Ambrose was skating across the ice, trying to keep his limbs as still as possible. He delighted in hearing nothing but the sound of his blades cutting into that gleaming sheet. There was no one else on the rink. He could take in sound without interruption, without competing noise. When his momentum slowed to a stop, he turned around and propelled himself once more in the opposite direction, churning his body until he reached maximum speed, then stopping all movement of his arms and legs, listening intently to the singular hiss of the skates.

In all his years of skating, he'd never before been alone on the ice. Invariably, he had found himself in the company of a family on a winter outing, a couple on a date, young hockey players chasing pucks, or someone just like him, methodically exercising as part of a health regimen.

On this night, however, Ambrose had awakened at 2:30 and had been unable to get back to sleep. He had planned for his usual Saturday midmorning exercise but decided he was wasting precious time staring at the ceiling and chose instead to tire himself on a rink before returning home to sleep away the morning hours.

He had left a note for his wife, who would just be ending her nursing shift at the hospital, and he'd driven the silent, empty streets to a rink at the edge of the neighborhood. Arriving shortly after 3 a.m., he'd been surprised to find someone seated near the ice, removing skates and slipping into winter boots. Someone else who couldn't sleep, Ambrose thought.

When that person was gone and Ambrose was alone, he felt a liberating thrill. A pick-up truck slowed down as it passed, and Ambrose pictured the driver studying him, wondering what kind of eccentric skates at this hour. In the stillness of the 10-degree air, Ambrose felt refreshed. He skated briskly around the rink, wondering why he'd never tried this before. He luxuriated in the freedom of having no one to skate around, slow down for, or even acknowledge. At times, he skated with his eyes closed, just because he could.

Employees of this small municipality had shut down most of the playground lights by 10 p.m., but they'd left one towering lamp blazing near the rink. Ambrose now wished that were off as well, so he could clearly see the full moon. A "snow moon" it was called in February. What would it be like, he thought, skating on some river tonight under that wistful moon out in the country away from any sounds or signs of civilization? He longed to experience it one time before the winter ended. He didn't care that the ice would be shoddy or need shoveling. He was falling in love with the dark, the quiet, and the solitude.

Ambrose stayed warm by moving. His long olive-green, wool coat came almost to his calves. His black earmuffs kept his thick, unruly dark hair in place, and his navy-blue scarf flopped like the tail of a kite. The frigid air made his skin ruddy and more aged than his 44 years, but his stamina on the rink was that of someone 10 years younger. No one watching him would have considered him a graceful skater. He moved with determined effort more than with ease, but his face was serene as he glided. This was more than weekly exercise tonight, he thought. This was enchantment.

The next vehicle coming down the street didn't slow down. In fact, it was speeding faster than was prudent on such a narrow, icy street. Ambrose heard the revving engine before he ever looked up to see the headlights. He lifted his head just in time to watch it swerve, barely missing a parked van, and spin into the boulevard, sending a plume of white powder into the air. Ambrose pulled up to the wooden boards framing the rink and held himself in place. The car had knocked over a stop sign and had come to rest on the sidewalk 25 yards from the rink. A heavy-set figure flung open the driver's-side door and ran from the vehicle, disappearing down an alley. Seconds later, two squad cars appeared, one from the front, one from the rear, red and blue lights flashing blindingly in the darkness. The policemen noticed Ambrose and yelled in his direction, asking if he'd seen where the driver had gone. Ambrose pointed and shouted, "That alley." One cop raced on foot, the other got back in his squad car and sped in the same direction.

Ambrose watched with astonishment. The night's meditative spell had been broken, startlingly. He was left to ponder the back story to this frantic spectacle. Was it a stolen car? Was it a drunk driver? Would he soon hear gunfire? Should he leave?

Then he heard the music. He hadn't noticed it in the immediate chaos, but now it was clear and booming, coming from the car. The driver's door of this vintage Mustang was wide open, and a speaker on the door was blaring classical music. Ambrose even recognized the piece. Bach's "Chaconne," a long violin solo heard at the end of Partita No. 2 in D minor. How odd, Ambrose thought. Would any car thief listen to classical music and at such an ear-piercing volume? Do the inebriated ever leave a bar blasting Bach on a stereo?

He thought about going up to the car and turning off the music. He could see exhaust coming from the tail pipe. Should he turn the key and kill the engine? Or was this a crime scene? Was he even allowed to touch anything? He figured the police would sort it out soon enough.

So instead, he began to skate once more, albeit slowly, and with uncertainty. The movement seemed to help relieve some of his agitation, but his tranquil sense of solitude was slow to return. He felt self-conscious. The skating felt awkward. He considered calling it a night. Moving quietly in a measured and wide circle, he kept his eyes on the car. But when no one seemed to be returning from the chase, he allowed himself to skate more fluidly, while still keeping watch. The car sat at an awkward angle, half on the sidewalk, half on the snowy boulevard, a stop sign resting on its hood.

His curiosity about the crime, if there had been one, and the ensuing chase, shifted to an interest in the music filling the night air. Gone was the isolated sound of skates on ice. But in its place was something else Ambrose could get lost in, an emotive violin solo in a mournful key. The music added a surreal element that he found absurd but appealing. He let out a quiet laugh. How ridiculous it was, he thought, to take in such a sublime sound under a full moon in the small hours of the morning through such a reckless, haphazard act. His evening of solitude now had a soundtrack, he mused. And not just any soundtrack, one of Bach's most famous compositions, written in the early 1700s, after the composer had returned home from a trip and learned his wife had died.

Ambrose studied classical music in graduate school and remembered this piece because it was one of the longest solos ever composed for a violin, and because another composer, Johannes Brahms, had once said that if he were to so much as imagine himself composing such a work, the earth-shattering power of it would "drive him out of his mind." Ambrose figured this was the finest compliment Bach had ever received.

He began to skate less like an aging athlete now and more like an awkward dancer, moving to the music in ways he'd never moved before. Occasionally, he'd look over at the car to see if anyone had returned. When he saw he was still alone, he moved with less inhibition, allowing his arms to rise above his head and sway with the sound. Then, turning around, he skated backwards in wide zigzags with his head held back and his arms outstretched like wings. He imagined himself at an Olympic performance in a choreographed routine in sync with the sweeping, soaring notes of a Stradivarius. Tears began to well in his eyes as he felt all the emotion in those somber, lustrous notes. The vibrating strings seemed to extend from the instrument straight to his chest, burrowing into his heart. He sensed the music falling through the air as ancient tears. A confluence of joy, sadness, and bewilderment moved though him in graceful swirls. What an astoundingly strange evening this had turned out to be, he thought.

He crouched down low, bending his knees as much as possible, resting his forearms on his thighs, and listening with deep concentration, allowing the sound to envelop him like a soft blanket.

He felt every note as a lingering caress. Then, as the soloist brought the violin higher in intensity and tempo, Ambrose rose in a burst of energy and propelled himself across the rink, muscling each movement in unison with the sound. He no longer thought of the car resting on the sidewalk. He'd stopped wondering if the police were ever coming back. He was lost in the score, one that seemed perfectly written for the darkness, and the shadows, and the penetrating cold.

Three miles north of the playground, near the front porch of Ambrose's one-story bungalow, a squad car was pulling up. A young officer, clutching a notepad, got out and walked to the front door. She knocked, shuffling her feet back and forth. When no one answered, the officer tried the doorbell, then retreated down the steps to wait on the sidewalk, tapping her notepad nervously on her palm. Still no response. The officer brought out her cell phone and slowly punched in the 10 digits that were written on her notepad.

At the playground, Ambrose was panting but beaming. He had taken off his scarf and earmuffs and was circling the rink slowly, in what felt to him like a state of grace. He felt held aloft by the currents of this haunting, holy sound, a sound that had left him pondering the paradox of deep pain and soothing comfort.

He didn't notice the police officer emerging from the nearby alley. The one who would soon turn off the music, shut down the engine, close the car door, and begin to take photographs of the hood and the windshield, bloodstained from the night's hit and run.

But Ambrose could feel the cell phone vibrating in his pocket.

The Little Things

"That man is richest whose pleasures are cheapest."
— **Henry David Thoreau**

Winter's charm is often in its small details and fleeting moments. Sure, it can offer grand pageantry, but many of its denizens treasure some far less showy aspects of the season. Some of these features, shared with others, bring a knowing smile. But other facets are so obscure they're cherished by a relative few.

I have come across people who strain to articulate why it's so pleasurable to step on frozen puddles that have formed after snow has melted and temps have then dropped again. I've offered a knowing nod as they've described the oddly satisfying sensation of the crunch of the ice breaking beneath them. I knew that peculiar pleasure as a child, and I can still find it today, though I also struggle to explain its mysterious appeal.

Everyone in the North Country can appreciate the beauty of a seemingly endless snow-covered farm field glowing peacefully beneath a full moon, but I can just as easily find myself in harmony with the person who is enamored with those moments, lying in bed, listening to the rumble of a city snowplow coming down the street in the middle of the night. I find myself fully in accord with their description of that deeply comforting sensation of being "cared for" by some stranger while they lie safe and warm beneath the blankets.

I don't know how many people can resonate with the nostalgic waves that can move through a person when listening to a distant shovel scraping across a sidewalk in the darkness of an early evening, but I can. The shoveler can't be seen, only heard. And if, by chance, you're also shoveling, making your own scraping sound, there is that peculiar sense of communion with the stranger. Perhaps everyone else in the neighborhood took care of clearing the snow in daylight hours, but you two waited until after supper. The night is clear, as it often is after a snowfall, and the houses glow, each in their own way, up and down the block. You are both engaged in an ancient custom that can no more be separated from this landscape than the very frost on the windows. In the darkness, a great distance may separate you two, but there's a sense of a signal moving back and forth, the sound of your shovel and the sound of theirs. A winter language is being spoken, in some foreign yet familiar tongue. And it too is oddly comforting.

Children could certainly add to this list of simple pleasures, and somewhere in the mix might be the wonder of peeing in the snow. When my boys were quite little, there were few delights that entertained them as much as this. Watching the snow instantly melt in whatever direction they aimed never failed to get them giggling. It wasn't long before they were creating artistic designs or attempting to spell out their full names. It might not be advice you get often, but I think everyone should pee in a fresh snowfall at least once in their lives.

My mother had winter memories from her childhood that involved some unorthodox pursuits. She and her siblings would routinely run around their snowy yard barefoot and then race back inside and stick their feet in buckets of cold water. She told me there were two reasons they found this so gratifying. One was the sheer absurdity of running around barefoot in the snow. It felt rebellious, dangerous, and exhilarating. The other reason was the puzzling sensation of feeling a warmth move through their bodies when sticking their feet in cold water. However cold that water was, it was far warmer than the snow had been, so the sensation was always one of relief and comfort. As kids, my mother said that they were dumbfounded and tickled by this.

The reason their parents allowed the practice, my mother said, was that it was considered good for one's health. She said the people of rural central Minnesota believed exposure to the cold gave a healthy boost to their vitality. For this reason, she encouraged my siblings and me to repeat this activity when we were kids, and I in turn had my children do the same. It never got old.

Another winter experience that will never get old is the comfort of a car that has been allowed to run and heat up before it needs to be driven. Being on top of things to such a degree that you remember to get your vehicle started long before you need to race off is the kind of heads-up move that pays welcome dividends. My personal pleasure is when my wife is late for an appointment and frantically gathering her things. It's five below zero and she's certain she's headed out to an ice box for an automobile. But I have secretly started and warmed the car for her, and I now stand near the second-floor window studying her reaction as she's enveloped in the surprise of 70 luxurious degrees. Northerners all know this sense of relief. Those first couple of miles won't feature tense muscles after all. The car is now a cozy den. The coffee will taste better, the radio will play sweeter, and the view out the window will be indulged, not cursed.

There are other thrills that are just as universal. There's the occasion, in the middle of a cold Northern winter, when suddenly, on a single day, the temperature will rise far above the average for that time of year. It may even break the record for that given day. This is the bewildering gift winter doles out, seemingly out of nowhere. Our bodies have been acclimated to the cold, so they now can feel comfortable in weather that would be unbearably chilly on a summer day. Consequently, it doesn't take much for a winter afternoon to feel balmy. Temps in the 40s can get one thinking of sidewalk cafes or a nearby park where throwing a Frisbee might seem appropriate. If it gets warmer still, people often won't know what to do with themselves. They'll slip into a seductively bemused, almost woozy state. There are but a few hours to take all of this in before Old Man Winter returns from his lunch break. The day screams for a momentous response.

My senior year in high school one such magical day appeared, and it still burns brightly in my memory four decades later. One month after the winter solstice has traditionally been the time when the North can register its coldest temperatures. The last two weeks of January have presented winter at its absolute harshest for generations.

So, the startling combination, in late January, of a record high temp, coinciding with the liberating arrival of a Saturday, resulted in an electrifying teenage sensation that I have rarely known since, and one that will forever give me a memory hard to adequately articulate, but exquisite to recall.

Fifty-seven degrees, the mercury read that afternoon, a temperature so farcical for January in Minnesota that my incredulous friends and I were inspired to don shorts and drag a keg of beer to a neighborhood soccer field, where we pranced about like it was mid-July. To our bodies it might as well have been 80 degrees. The shirts came off, the sweat poured, and, as we kicked the soccer ball around, we swore we all got sunburned. I remember someone had a boombox playing, and the rock and roll completed the picture of kids who had already graduated and were now living free in some endless summer. And it all unfolded on glorious Saturday, the schoolboy's blessed furlough from the drudgery of the classroom.

Monday morning, walking to school, it was overcast and cold once again. But that Saturday afternoon carried us like a dream right into spring. It was as if we all had received that winter break to Florida that our parents could never afford. It made the rest of the winter fly by.

There is now a temptation for someone to ask, if such a day were so welcome, why wouldn't one want a year of them? But that question betrays an ignorance to the way life's greatest pleasures are only felt in the greatest of contrasts. It is precisely because January is typically so bitingly cold that this day is still celebrated decades later. It wouldn't have meant anywhere near as much had it happened in late March. It would have been forgotten in a week. In fact, it could never mean the same thing in most other regions of the country.

There are, I suspect, many fine stories from that improbable Saturday. Somewhere, there's a person who remembers being stuck working indoors that day. They had never smoked a cigarette in their life but pretended to be cursed with the habit that afternoon, as they borrowed a smoke from a coworker just to acquire a reason to slip out beneath the eves, their head up and their eyes closed, feeling the massage of warm air that hadn't been around since the colored leaves were falling. Somewhere there's a person who was miserably sick with a head cold that day but couldn't stop themselves from jubilantly strutting out the front door, convinced the weather by itself would cure them. Of course, somewhere else there were those who honestly lamented this disconcerting warmth. The cold was preferable. It's where they were happiest. These are the true followers of Boreas, the certified winter people, and they are a breed unto themselves.

Winter's Disciples

"You can't get too much winter in the winter."
— **Robert Frost**

There is a common take found in most of the media that a warm sunny day with rustling leaves in the trees and the presence of emerald grass accented with colorful flowers represents a kind of ideal. In film, television, or magazines, it's the outdoor environment most celebrated for coming closest to a type of aesthetic perfection. Ask people to take a few colored markers and rapidly draw their image of paradise, and some similar tableau will appear, maybe with an ocean beach thrown in. It's our default utopia. But, while most Northerners won't argue with the beauty, comfort, and serenity of such a scene, there are some who would take issue with the claim that it's the pinnacle.

There is no one-size-fits-all offering when it comes to the way the natural world can sooth, delight, and inspire. I know cold-weather diehards who share a passion for winter that would confound people in most other parts of the country. Northern native Dinah Lillestrand, for instance, feels her greatest sense of relief, not when the March snow melts and the air warms, but when the cold finally arrives in December. The joy many others express with the welcoming of spring she reserves for the darkest of days.

"The first time everything is covered in snow I suddenly feel so good," she told me. "I absolutely love snow. It's so beautiful to me. I love the cold air; I love the smell of the air after a snowfall. I actually start to get a little depressed when spring comes around. I'll take extreme cold so much more than heavy heat. It's not even a contest. My energy level goes up the colder it gets. I even love the darkness of winter. People associate the short days with depression, but it's just the opposite for me. I love those days. I love the way the darkness closes out the day early and you feel like you can now relax, the day is over. The darkest of winter is when I'm happiest. When the sun goes down, I feel there's nothing more I'm supposed to do. When it's light out in the summer till nine o'clock at night, I feel this pressure that I should be out doing something. Everyone is outside running around, and the world loses that feeling of peacefulness."

Eric Anderson is another Northerner who uses language typically reserved for spring to describe his passion for the winter season.

"At the end of the fall, when the first snow comes, it's like a renewal. Late in fall, after all the leaves are off the trees, it's just dull and bleak. But then all of a sudden that first snowfall comes, and it just brightens everything up. And it opens a whole new world of possibilities for the things one can do. The ground underneath is going to sleep, and this whole new beautiful world is coming to life. We can get out and enjoy it in so many ways, hiking on snowy trails, cross-country skiing, snowshoeing. It's wonderful. And everybody seems to go back out when the snow falls. The world kind of comes back to life."

Sandra Darrow told me winter leaves her "awestruck." Whatever the climate has offered in the other three seasons, her deepest sense of wonderment is reserved for winter

"It's Mother Nature putting on an amazing display for all of us and showing us how powerful she is. It is seasonal drama. It is humbling. It can stop us in our busy lives and make us take notice. And I love how people hunker down when the winter gets real extreme and how there will be this unity that develops with one's community. Winter draws people closer to one another."

Sandra said that for her winter is "the great reset." The seasons have a way of marking off time, she says, and winter is like nature's coda.

"Elsewhere in the country where the seasons are not so starkly defined, the months can just kind of bleed into one another and you can lose the sense of passing time in a way you don't in a northern winter. Winter provides this time for a kind of forced re-evaluation. The darkness and the cold always spark creativity for me. It opens a door. My mind wanders more freely. Even the quality of light, which is so different in winter, has a way of inspiring me. As does the quiet. The incredible silence after a fresh snow is hard to find outside of winter. I can be inspired by other seasons but nothing like what happens to me in the winter."

Mac Meade is also enamored with the North's winter silence. It has almost a mystical effect on him. "There's simply no silence like the silence of one of those crystal-cold winter nights," he said. "It's very hard for me to describe the effect this has on me, but I just crave it. Everything is stone silent and crystal clear. Everything is so pure and clean and crisp. There's just something about it that I love. A tradition for me every year is to find the night that I think is going to be the absolute coldest night of the year and I walk out in the darkness and stand in the middle of a frozen lake. I just stand there. There's an intensity that I experience there that I just can't experience any other time. I really don't know how to explain it."

Kerry Pederson told me when she was younger, she detested winter, but in her older years she finds a "quiet serenity" in the darkness. She said it's as if winter gives her permission to do nothing.

"I love how in the winter I can slow down. I can just look out the window and watch the snow fall or look up at the stars. Nothing more. Winter brings a lack of urgency to life. The older I get the more I like the slowing down that winter brings. During all my married life, we were always busy, always doing something. Every morning I would hit the ground running. But my kids grew older, and my husband died, and now winter suits me. It grows so quiet in the winter. It's the opposite of the craziness of life in the summer."

Jack Pavlik told me he takes an almost perverse pride in his love of winter's darkness. "I must have a sadistic streak in me because I secretly love hearing people talk about how much they hate the days growing so short, while I'm thriving on all that early darkness. For me, it just really focuses my mind." Jack said there's something wildly appealing about the dramatic shifts winter presents, the way the whole world can change in appearance overnight. And like others, he is taken with the silence after a fresh snowfall. But more than just the silence, he says he's "fascinated by the way sound behaves so differently in the cold." On a quiet winter night, a far-off sound that couldn't be heard in the summer is picked up in the dense cold air. Cold air slows down the speed of sound, but it makes sound travel farther. And because the quality of any sound is related to what it's bouncing off, sound buffered by snow has its own unique qualities.

"I think the start of a new year should come with the start of winter," Jack said. "That feels more like the fresh start of something. Spring doesn't even feel like as fresh of a start. Winter comes, and it's like you've put a fresh coat of paint inside a new house and now you are all ready to move in. It's this clear fresh beginning where everything else can now follow."

Carol Arend talked about "leaning into" the darkness of a Northern winter. Far from bringing her down, she views it as an invitation.

"I've come to view the darkness as a real gift because of the way it presents me with an opportunity for contemplation," she said. "It's as though winter is giving me this chance to just be, rather than do. And for me winter is a time to think differently. I'm not someone who's necessarily that great at thinking outside the box, but winter seems to encourage rethinking things and reevaluating. And the short days make the environment conducive for that. I love to light candles for breakfast in the morning when it's still dark outside. There's nothing quite like the feeling that gives me. There are just opportunities here that don't exist the rest of the year.

"I used to be a real winter baby. I didn't do well in the cold. But then I married a man who loved the outdoors. He's one of these 'there is no bad weather, only bad clothing' kind of guys. His family all loved winter. So, I decided I needed to start getting out there, forcing myself to engage with it. I made a commitment to take a winter walk every day. And it changed my view. The night after a snowstorm is my favorite time to walk. Having that clear sky and that fresh snow. Everything seems brittle, and there's this incredible quiet. It's stunningly beautiful."

Carol said there's no getting around the fact that some things get harder in the winter. Snow and cold can bring "hassles" to her life and make demands that are absent in a summer existence. But, she said, there's even something strangely appealing about that.

"Winter makes me tougher, and I like that. I'm a small woman and I'm not very strong, but when I come out of a Northern winter, I feel tougher. I feel like I rose to some challenge, and that makes me feel good."

Bill Quinn spent 27 years going to battle against the Northern winter's biggest storms. As an airport snowplow operator, he relished the blizzards that would envelop his world.

"The worse the storm, the more excited I got," he said. "I just loved being out in it. I've always had a high tolerance for cold weather. I'm now retired, but I like to get out and ski and snowshoe, and I have a fat tire bike that I ride all winter long.

"But now I also appreciate the quietness of winter. I like to go out and order a glass of wine some place and just stare out the window at the snow falling. And I love watching the sun go down in the winter and seeing what the light does. There's this point, as the sun goes down, where the snow seems to turn this iridescent blue. It's only for a few minutes, but it's just beautiful. I don't know what makes it do that, but it's one of my favorite times of the day."

Corey Wilson shares Bill's passion for the coldest months.

"I can't wait for that first snowfall, she told me. "Just the way the light comes through the blinds when that white is coming down makes me happy. And when I walk over and pull open the blinds completely and I see the brand new winter, right there before me, I'm ecstatic.

"I know this sounds strange but, just walking outside after a snowfall, even just out to the garage, and making those first footprints in the snow, being the first person to step on it, I don't know what it is, but it's such a wonderful feeling to me.

"I still have this memory of being a young girl in a snowy field and letting myself fall backwards, landing in the soft snow and looking up at the snowflakes coming down, all of them glowing from nearby streetlamps. There was this feeling that I was in a snow globe. It was such a magical thing. That way of being with nature for me has such a stronger effect on me than being with nature in the summer. In the summer, the natural world is almost too busy for me. The peacefulness and the quiet of the outdoors in winter does something to me that's far more powerful.

"People talk about nature in winter as being dead but I never understand that. It's alive. It's just taking a different form. And I so appreciate the beauty of that different form.

"For friends, I tend to gravitate to people who prefer winter over summer. When I'm around people who are getting excited because the winter is fading and the sun is staying up in the sky later in the day, I can't join in. I'm just bummed. I'm anticipating the summer when I'll be down the way other people can be down in the dark months."

Corey called winter, "an introvert's paradise." She told me she relishes the way snow can quiet the land, providing a sound buffer, but at the same time allowing in a single sound from some great distance, like that of a far-off train whistle, a sound that than sits isolated and highlighted in the auditory landscape. For her, summers are loud in comparison, throwing too much into the environment. She said there's an internal version of this as well.

"Winter not only has a way of quieting the outside, but it also has a way of quieting things inside you. It has a way of taking out the white noise in a person's head and clearing the way for the mind to focus on a single thing, contemplatively. It has a way of bringing out what's in your soul."

Justin Ayd may be the most extreme example of a person best suited for winter life. In fact, he may be better suited for the Arctic.

"When summer hits, I'm just counting the days until fall," Justin told me. "I'm at my lowest in the summer. The season just leaves me depressed. And it's right after autumn, when winter finally hits, that I'm most content, most at peace, and feel the greatest sense of well-being. And I'm not an outdoors sports enthusiast or into outdoor activities. A walk in the cold is pretty much it for me. It's more about the feel of the season itself. I prefer it over every other season. It's when I feel most alive. That's just how I'm built. I feel the best creatively, and I feel the best emotionally, in the winter.

"I think one thing that really suits me about winter is the way it seems to slow down time. The slow crawl of winter is what I appreciate. I have to say I'm unapologetically bothered by people going on and on about how much they love the summer, the long days, and warm temperatures. I couldn't be more the opposite. When winter comes, I feel I can breathe. And I thrive. In fact, if you want me to paint an ideal winter scenario, it's me snowed in at a cabin in the woods. A blizzard is coming down all around me and I can't see anything out the window but white, can't see a neighboring property, can't see another soul. Just the swirling white out there. I am in the cabin in my own private bubble. In that situation, I feel myself completely decompress. I feel myself recharge. I feel centered. I guess the warm summer months are sensory overload for me. There's just too much going on in the environment. It fills me with anxiety."

John Dee told me he moved to the North from his native Chicago because the winter's there were too weak. He went in search of a far more intense winter experience and found his empire of snow in Michigan's Upper Peninsula. There was four feet on the ground the day he visited, and he says he had almost a religious experience.

"I said right then and there, this is where I want to be. First, because I just find snow so beautiful, but more than that, I actually find it therapeutic. The more snow that falls, the better my mood. I honestly get a little sad when a particular snowfall ends, even if it's one that has already delivered two feet of snow, which can often happen up here."

John said as he watches snow fall, he can feel any anxiety he might be experiencing instantly dissolve. And if he witnesses a major snowstorm, "a real wild blizzard," that peaceful calm will get upgraded to a giddy delight.

"Not too long after I arrived here, I remember coming back from a nighttime snowmobile ride after a huge snowfall, and both of my dogs were there waiting for me. Rather than go inside to warm up, I couldn't help just playing with them in all that white, just frolicking in that snow like we were three little kids having a blast, rolling around in all of it. I thought to myself, this is as close to heaven as I'm ever going to get. In that kind of snow, I'm in my glory."

John said he's become something of a "Pied Piper of snow." He's now a professional meteorologist who maintains an online weather journal, and he said he knows many people from places farther south who started out just enjoying his weather writing but who eventually made the move to his adopted home in the Keweenaw Peninsula, basking in monster snowfalls unmatched in all but a few parts of the country.

"These people are what I call 'snow converts.' They've come to know and to embrace these same extraordinary winters that I've been enamored with for most of my life."

Snowflake Bentley

"How full of the creative genius is the air in which these snowflakes are generated! I should hardly admire more if real stars fell and lodged on my coat. Nature is full of genius, full of the divinity, so that not a snowflake escapes its fashioning hand."
— **Henry David Thoreau**

For countless numbers of people living in the Northland in the late 19th century, snow was seen as frozen flecks dropping from the sky. One man gets credit for altering this prosaic view and replacing it with the realization that each flake is an utterly unique work of geometric art.

Wilson Bentley spent his entire life intrigued by snowflakes. In an era when photography was still primitive, he figured out a way to use a microscope with a camera to capture the graceful and seemingly infinite variety of designs in individual flakes, something no one had ever done before. And he didn't just photograph a few. He took pictures of thousands of snowflakes, year after year, for decades. He would wander a field during a snowfall with a sheet of black velvet, catching the flakes and gingerly isolating certain ones with the gentle push of a feather.

Snowflakes fueled his imagination from childhood onward. No one he knew gave them a second thought, but Wilson saw them as a miracle, a secret window into the beauty and mystery of the world.

As he grew older, many would stare at him dismissively as he spent hours in the Vermont cold, studying the tiny flakes. Most thought he was foolishly wasting his time, especially his father and brother, who would have preferred he get busy helping them with the farm work. But in every snowflake Wilson was able to place under his microscope, he saw a mesmerizing work of artistic expression, and he knew he had to share this discovery with the world. Using light-sensitive glass plates, he delivered portrait after portrait of individual snowflakes to people who had no idea of the intricate, complex, and symmetrical designs each flake presented.

In the 19th century, Vermont farmers dreaded winter, but Wilson longed for it. It brought back his passion, though one that delivered no financial reward. In fact, it cost him money. After many failed and frustrating attempts, Wilson took his first successful snowflake photograph in 1885. It left him ecstatic. Forty-six years and 5,000 photographs later, he was finally able to get a publisher to formally present his pictures in a book. He placed his aging 66-year-old hands on a fresh copy for the very first time, just after Thanksgiving, 1931, days before he would come down with pneumonia, and less than a month before he would die.

I often think of Wilson when I stand at the window during a snowfall. I think of the excitement he felt when those first snow crystals would appear in the sky and the extraordinary efforts he would make to capture them, staying out in the cold for hours so he could photograph them without them melting, carefully moving them to his camera and microscope device with a straw drawn from a broom. For close to half a century, he never tired of this. He never lost his amazement at the way the snowflakes could all be so different. I imagine him at his window watching a snowfall and realizing that graceful intricate designs that no one would ever see and appreciate were slipping away. He knew each snowfall brought breathtaking art never before encountered: fresh, mysterious creations, born anew, snowfall after snowfall, winter after winter. He must have lived his life in a state of reverence and wonderment. That some people thought he was wasting his time makes one wonder what people hope for from their existence. If the chance to live a life ceaselessly charmed and entranced by the mystery of the earth's intricate beauty was a waste, what was the proper way to spend those years?

Wilson's greatest gift, in my view, was his ability to take the sense of wonder that he felt as a 10-year-old, when he first became interested in snowflakes, and carry that with him into adolescence, young adulthood, and finally old age. Few hang on to that ability to innocently marvel at the world, not because they don't want to, but because it's gradually stripped from them in the process of growing up.

I've learned many lessons from the man they called "Snowflake Bentley." I've learned that winter is such a rich, inspiring, and vastly rewarding season that one can take the smallest part of it, a single snowflake, and devote a lifetime to celebrating its delicate presentation. I've learned to look at winter from more perspectives, with greater patience and more openness and amazement. And I've been reminded why our world owes a debt of gratitude to the outsiders, the eccentrics, the brave ones who follow a path few around them admire at the time.

Because of Wilson Bentley, I have become interested in learning more about snow. I've learned simple things, like how it's not white but translucent. Light doesn't pass through snowflakes as it would with a window, but instead reflects off them, and then scatters in all directions. It's the way light is reflected that makes snow appear white.

Jon Nelson, a cloud physicist at Ritsumeikan University in Kyoto, Japan, estimates that the number of snowflakes that fall to earth each year is more than a quadrillion, quintillion, or sextillion. It's in the neighborhood of a septillion. He says, consequently, "the sheer variety in snowflake shapes, over time, exceeds the number of atoms in the universe."

I grew up believing the native people of Alaska had more words for snow than could be found in any other culture. But I've learned that it is, in fact, the Scottish native tongue that offers the most nuanced take on snow. They have a name for snow that swirls around a corner and snow that's half liquid and floats upon a river. "Flindrikin" is a light snow shower, "flukra" is snow falling in large flakes, "spitters" are small flakes in a wind-driven snowfall, drifting snow is known as "blin-drift," melting snow is "glush," melted snow is "snaw-broo," and a large snowflake is a "skelf." Scottish academics believe there are more than 400 different words describing snow, including the word for ghosts who only appear in the snow, "snaw-ghast."

If I had never encountered Wilson Bentley's story, I would not have spent so much time learning about snow in all its many facets. Those efforts have added immeasurably to my appreciation for this centerpiece of winter life in the North Country. This newfound level of wonder and delight is the perspective that carried Wilson through all his years on this Earth. He forever deepened and enriched the meaning of the simple phrase "winter wonderland."

Celia

"I talk to trees and animals. We have interesting conversations about food, weather, and love."
— **Shan Sa, novelist and painter**

In some urban neighborhoods or in rural farming communities up North, one can occasionally find durable old residents known for their winter folk wisdom. They come across as having spent their many years pondering the elements, studying the seasons, meditating on nature, and by doing so, acquiring secret knowledge the rest of us missed along the way.

Our neighborhood has Celia. She lives alone in a cracker-box house near the railroad tracks and, in the cold months, is seen only when she emerges to shovel her long narrow walkway. She seems too frail for such a task but refuses aid of any kind. She dresses in mismatched clothing from what seems like a bygone era and keeps her stark white hair pulled back tightly, held in place with a cadre of bobby pins. Her light olive skin is wrinkled in the finest of symmetrical lines, so uniform in appearance they seem to have always been there. She has not an ounce of fat on her five-foot, three-inch frame, and her penetrating green eyes argue for her wisdom long before she ever opens her mouth.

"Celia sees stuff the rest of us don't," my older brother is fond of saying. And she routinely proves it.

"Did you notice the woolly bear caterpillar this past fall?" she'll ask. "The brown band in the middle was thin as can be. That signals a harsh winter ahead."

Having never studied this connection, or any such relationship, we don't know whether to believe her or not. That is, until we meet those piercing green eyes. They seem to place exclamation points all around her raspy words, and we feel as though, even if what she's saying isn't accurate, it ought to be.

"When you cut open a wild plum, the size of the seed often tells you if the winter will be cold or mild," Celia says. "And if it's spoon-shaped, you can expect plenty of snow."

I'm sure people like her used to be commonplace. The dispensing of folk wisdom must have been the norm way back when. But now such individuals seem rare, and their utterances come across as ancient readings from a book of fairy tales.

"The date of the first snowflakes plus the number of days past the new moon will indicate how many times it will snow this winter."

I'm tempted to make a joke whenever Celia talks this way, but those haunting eyes keep me in line. Besides, I've never worked that hard doing the research to prove her wrong. Nevertheless, while part of me wants to believe her every word, I have the sense that some of her utterances are about as accurate as your average advertising slogan.

"When squirrels early start to hoard, winter will pierce us like a sword."

I'm aware the animal world is gifted with extensions of the senses we've lost, or perhaps never attained. And there are people wiser than I who read the natural world like a doctor studying a health chart. And I don't doubt, as Celia says, that watching a beaver build an unusually large and sturdy den could be an indication they've tapped into some impending seasonal shift that we're not attuned to. And yes, if their coats grow thicker than usual, and if they double up on their food caches, we ought to take notice. But part of me wants to ask, what does it really matter? In our modern world, how will any of this change the way we move forward with our winter day? We still grab our coffee thermos, warm up the car engine, and drive to work with the radio on, same as always. It's a modern era. I'm not sure we still need warning flags from the rodent world.

My brother, however, says it doesn't matter if we need such insights or not; we need charmingly eccentric neighbors like Celia. He says they bring much needed color to our spare winter world and remind us of the interconnectedness of all living things. Whether what she says is gospel isn't important; she gets us thinking about things we otherwise wouldn't and noticing a world we too often ignore. Plus, Celia connects us to another era, when people didn't discuss the new cable TV series and whether or not a season finale lived up to expectations. They talked about the living world pulsating all around them.

"As high as the hornets build their nests so will the snow be this winter. You can take that to the bank," Celia tells me, her eyes never blinking, and her index finger raised high in the air as if willing the statement true with the wave of a wand.

"I didn't notice the hornets building their nests, this year," I say, but she tells me she made a point of it. Just like she kept checking the thickness of the apple skins as she pulled the ripened fruit from her backyard tree in early September.

"Those skins were thick as leather this year. Hunker down. The winter will be a doozy."

Well, they all are, of course, in one way or another. Fascinating, complex, and mysterious, no matter which version we're offered. It's theater either way, ushering in a cast of stars, walk-ons, cameos, extras, as well as transcendent scenes and settings impossible for any artist to reproduce. It's a tantalizing spectacle, always, and all the natural forces have a role in its presentation, from each frigid breeze to the strands of DNA in the finest hair of a slumbering red fox.

And that grand spectacle includes Celia, abruptly stopping her morning shoveling to listen to the staccato beat of a nearby woodpecker. With her eyes closed she counts off the hard pecks at the bark on the silver maple hanging over her house. It's just a knocking sound to the rest of us. It's a bulletin to Celia.

"Do you hear that?" she asks, as her eyes grow wide. "Things are going to start warming up around here."

We never ask her, afterword, if matters proceeded as predicted. And come spring, she's quickly on to other pursuits, equally unique. She gets busy burying plastic buckets in her backyard, up to their lips, and filling them with water and a few goldfish. She says she wants to create a "fishing experience" for the urban raccoons who come out after dusk scrounging for food.

"The raccoon world doesn't present the way it used to," she laments. "But we can give them a taste of how things used to be."

Which is exactly what Celia gives us all, a taste of the way things used to be. And we're going to miss her when she's gone.

The Therapist
and the Snowman

- a winter fantasy -

"Be content with what you have. Rejoice in how things are. When you realize there is nothing lacking, the whole world belongs to you."
— **Lao Tzu**

"I'm not much of a doer, Doc. Never been the 'get things done' type."

The snowman paused, gauging his therapist's reaction. He could see she was listening, but she said nothing; so he continued.

"This old fella with a funny accent told me, a couple weeks back, that there are those in this world who do and those who are content to just be. I told him there needs to be a third category, because while I never do, I'm not content to just be either. I mean, seriously, you think you've had some clients stuck in a rut, Doc? Have 'em talk to me. They don't know ruts. Look at me. I exist. That's it. I'm like those stroke victims with locked-in syndrome who can't move a muscle, not even form a facial expression, but their minds are perfectly fine. That's the story of my life."

The therapist made a couple of notes on her legal pad, then gently set it down in the snow beside her.

"I see a role for you that maybe you don't see," she said, adjusting the hood of a sleek, shiny parka. "Or, perhaps, one you don't appreciate. You are the neighborhood's great observer, it seems to me, the one who sees all, quietly and dispassionately. No one else in this area takes on that role. All the rest are busy living lives. You're busy taking in the living of those lives. Those are two very different vantage points, and each brings its own advantages, and both perspectives are valuable."

The snowman's response was deadpan. "Did you pick that up in shrink school? Handy talking points for stroke victims, quadriplegics, and snowmen?"

"That's not quite how it works," the therapist replied, calmly. "Each person is unique. No one approach works across the board. In this case, I just wondered whether your despondency wasn't a case of perspective. You were focusing on all you can't do and not on what you can."

"Says the woman who just returned from a ski trip to Vail. How was vacation, Doc? I'm realizing, suddenly, I should have sought the advice of another snowman. Someone who doesn't just talk the talk, but walks the, ...well someone with credibility."

"What emotions are coming up for you right now?" the therapist asked, removing her reading glasses and placing them in her pocket.

"Emotions?" the snowman said, raising his voice. "Emotions, Doc? Oh, I'd say anger, primarily. Yeah, that's it, anger."

"That's good," the therapist said. "But there's often an emotion behind anger. Anger usually protects a more vulnerable part of the self. Can you spend a moment trying to identify another emotion, one that's deeper?"

The snowman took a deep breath and exhaled forcefully, saying nothing. He stared off into the distance, into a yard across the street where neighbor kids were pulling a sled as a wiry terrier ran beside them, barking and nipping at their heels. In the windows of the bungalows that lined the avenue, he saw amber lights begin to glow in the late afternoon twilight. The therapist sat with her hands on her lap, one mitten on top of the other. Her legs were crossed at the ankles, and she stared intently into the snowman's charcoal eyes. Finally, he spoke.

"The person who made me never came back..."

The therapist listened for more, but there was silence. "Can you talk about that?" she asked.

"The person who made me on that snowy Saturday afternoon never returned to enjoy my presence, never brought others to look at me. I was created and left. Discarded. I was good for about a half hour of snow sculpting and then became an afterthought."

The therapist spoke softly. "Yes, I can see where that would be very painful."

The snowman continued. "I couldn't understand what the point of making me was if you weren't going to hang around."

"You no doubt felt rejected," the therapist said. "I imagine you were grateful to exist, but you hoped others would be grateful you existed, as well."

"It's bigger than that, Doc. Everybody needs some purpose. What was I there for? If it was important enough to make me, wasn't it important to give me a task? How do I bring joy when no one comes around to see me?

"You know how the song 'Frosty the Snowman' starts, Doc? 'Frosty the Snowman was a jolly happy soul.' A jolly happy soul? Really? How'd he pull that off? Well, listen to the rest of the song. The lucky bastard was somehow given a magic top hat that allowed him to dance and play with children. Show me a song about a happy snowman that doesn't involve a magic top hat. There aren't any. Honest snowmen songs would be dirges that speak of a short, lonely life and slow, painful death. That's the hard truth, Doc."

The therapist rubbed her forehead and looked down at her notepad in the snow. She brushed some falling flakes from her face and pulled her scarf tighter around her neck.

"What if I told you this yard that you're in is a more beautiful yard because of your existence? Without you, it's just snow on top of grass. But with you, it's come to life. It suddenly has personality. What if I told you cars that drive through this neighborhood may have drivers who only notice you for a fleeting moment, but in that moment, you remind them of their childhood, when they were happiest, and there's a slight but perceptible smile that comes across some of their faces? What if I told you the person who made you could have done anything with that Saturday afternoon? He could have gone skating or sledding or just stayed inside and played video games. But he thought it was important to work on creating you, carefully finding the right branches for your arms and the right carrot for your nose, even going so far as to search the attic for his grandfather's old pipe. He took care making you what you are. It must have mattered to him. He must have enjoyed that. Your birth must have brought him pleasure. That was your gift to him. That was your purpose."

"You're trying to earn your fee now, aren't ya, Doc."

The therapist picked up on the momentum and spoke noticeably louder.

"You're a snowman. A perfect snowman. Your purpose is to be yet another feature of this season, one that sharply separates it from all the other seasons."

She stood up and slipped into an orator's cadence.

"You are a snowman because you get to be, because winter allows it, it practically demands it, by dropping that sticky white stuff by the bucket load and setting it before the human imagination. You are part of the creative movement of the universe. It's as simple as that. You're here for a spell and then gone, just like the rest of us, playing your role and moving on, caught in the net of existence for one fleeting flash of life's mysterious dance. Your purpose is to be what you are, sure as any tulip, butterfly, or child."

"Reel it in, Doc. I need a therapist, not a date for Saturday."

The therapist sat down, invigorated but blushing. The Snowman's tone softened.

"I'm missing the larger picture, Doc. I get it. Or at least for this session, I get it. Whether it lasts, who knows? But then, I'm not here for that long. Fact is, you only need to keep me sane till late March. But I appreciate what you're saying. And I'll have to meditate on it.

"Did I tell you I've been trying some meditation? That same old fella who talked to me about 'doing' vs. 'being' gave me a sales pitch on meditation. In the country where he's from they apparently sit still for hours at a time and just rest in the awareness of their existence without getting carried away by their thoughts. He told me the most advanced meditators can spend days sitting still, and yet they claim to be in a state of continuous bliss. Good lord, can you think of any activity better suited to a snowman? I mean what are my hobby options? I was born to be a yogi, was I not?"

"That's wonderful to hear," the therapist said. "That's a real change in perspective right there. And I think it shows genuine progress. But I am sorry to say our time is up for today. We could certainly continue this at next week's session if you'd like."

"Oh, I'll be here, Doc. Ain't going nowhere; promise you that. But before you leave, could I ask a quick favor? I don't think that kid carved much of a smile on my face. Would you mind fixing that? I figure that's more or less what I'm paying for."

Winter's Laugh

"A lot of people like snow. I find it to be an unnecessary freezing of water."
— **Carl Reiner, comedian and screenwriter**

Winter is funny. I don't mean funny as in odd, though it's certainly that, but funny as in slapstick, slip-on-a-banana-peel funny. In fact, each winter, a kind of variation on the banana peel is laid on the ground in all directions. One could conclude the entire season is an elaborate prank, designed by that ornery god of winter himself. If so, you have to hand it to Boreas. The man knows how to entertain himself.

What's he doing when the rest of us are falling ass over tea kettle on icy sidewalks, parking lots, alleyways, and street corners? Is it one big cosmic guffaw, or has he become a serious student of the slip and fall, analyzing the nuances in each and every tumble? One leg shooting right, one arm going wildly skyward, a hand reaching desperately for the ground, lightning-speed calculations determining if there's enough snow to buffer the landing or if the angle of the descent means a more serious injury this time around.

And after the fall, is he howling with mischievous delight as we quickly complete the 360-degree scan, checking to see if anyone witnessed our graceless ballet? Does he know we're immediately thinking about our age? Are we old enough to be pitied, or are we young enough that they're merely embarrassed for us? We know we're no longer kids when falls would have been water off a duck's back, when we wouldn't have given a hoot who was watching, and when our spill would have had less to do with careless footsteps and more to do with our friend sneaking up behind us to get on all fours while his accomplice moved to the front and pushed us over. By the way, were they pulling that prank back in the Neolithic era? I hope so. Merriment diversions were limited. Maybe that's where it all started. Either way, just ask the kids, it never gets old.

From a certain perspective, it's difficult to think of a season more farcical than winter. Truckloads of snow randomly dumped on people's heads; there's absurdity right there. Rain could be viewed in a similar manner, but rain dries up quickly; snow and ice stick around to keep the comedy coming. In winter, the snow will occasionally melt a bit, then freeze solid once more, this time turning into something sinister. That's when the A-list hilarity ensues. You're late for work and racing from your house with a piece of toast in your mouth, a mug of coffee in your hand, and a briefcase under your arm. You awkwardly grab the car door handle, but it won't open. You fumble for your keys but soon realize the car door isn't locked, it's frozen shut. In frustration, you pull hard on the handle, but too hard, and it breaks. You're sent backward, barely able to maintain your balance and now wearing the coffee you had intended to drink. Another winter day has begun in the Northland, and it's a day thousands of others have known. It's not even worth passing along to your co-workers. It's garden-variety winter happenstance.

Ice dams are comical as well. Southern schadenfreude fans might buy tickets to watch hapless Northerners deal with their ice dams. Snow builds up on rooftops and the warmth of the house melts the bottom layer, sending water down to the eaves, the coldest part of the roof. There, the water freezes, slowly building a dam. More water melts higher up the roof and slides down under the snowpack. Soon, the melting snow has nowhere to go but into the home. Plastic buckets and saucepans are set out to catch it all. The lily-white ceiling now develops a spreading yellow-brown stain. The do-it-yourself homeowner heads up to the roof to deal with the problem, armed with extension cords, space heaters, and hair dryers. That's where the high comedy is born. Okay, it's not funny watching someone topple off an extension ladder, or get electrocuted, or slide down a roof into the open air, but it's entertaining watching people come up with do-it-yourself approaches to battling winter, knowing that, just like the Road Runner, winter will win every time.

One winter, I wanted to build my own backyard ice rink. I thought it would encourage the kids to learn to skate. I read that it was best to lay down a huge sheet of plastic across the backyard and to tack it to two-by-six boards, which could form the frame of the rink, keeping the water pooling in place so it could freeze. Night after night I stood out there under the stars with a hose, flooding the area, feeling a Northlander's pride. This is how you take on winter, I thought—you get creative, and you make it work for you, not against you.

The cold nights passed, and the flooding continued. It was tedious work, and I got cold and wet, but I told myself it would all be worth it.

I'd never bothered to investigate how long it should take to flood a rink sufficiently. Multiple nights didn't seem unusual; there was a lot of territory to cover. But after more than a week, I felt something was wrong. There was not the solid sheet I'd hoped for. It didn't look right. This is when I learned there was a tear in the plastic tarp and on an end of my property that dipped, precipitously. Beyond it, there was a steady slope that went under a picket fence and on into my neighbor's yard. Suffice it to say I ruined the winter for her dog, who ordinarily loved a good romp around her backyard but didn't love sliding uncontrollably, legs splayed, eyes filled with terror, fur bouncing off fence pickets and careening into pine trees. Yes, I'd made a fine ice rink all right, but not in my yard, in hers, and not just in part of her yard. The whole thing was a glacier.

I swear to you I didn't emit a single giggle that season, watching her slide, cuss, scream, and tumble her way to her garage each morning. Others might have, but I was an adult. In fact, I was mature enough to deliver a heartfelt apology card, along with a brand-new pair of ice skates. Later, I spotted the skates sailing over the picket fence and landing on my garage roof. Must have been the wrong size.

Now, unlike my neighbor, I've never had that icy walk from a house to a nearby garage to fetch my vehicle, because I've always been a park-on-the-street type of guy. Many people don't have the use of a garage in the cold season, and their cars are always the easy ones to spot after a snowfall. Depending on how hurried they were clearing the snow, their vehicles can appear as four-wheeled snow cones coming down the roadway, the white stuff piled up everywhere but on the windshield. The real slackers scrape little more than a rectangular slit in the glass, leaving the car otherwise buried in snow and creating the image of a lumbering arctic tank. The lack of clear sightlines for the driver means these cars present a serious danger to anyone nearby. I should know; I've often been the one behind the wheel.

I drove a vintage VW Karmann Ghia for a couple of winters, possibly the most impractical winter car in all of the Northland. The windows were small to begin with so there was no excuse for not clearing them completely. But I'd occasionally be just that lazy and leave nothing but a periscope-size opening for navigation. I was pulled over by a cop for such incompetence on one occasion, and he walked up to my snow-covered windows determined to write me a ticket for careless driving. He didn't end up giving me the ticket, however. An unexpected discovery had him laughing too hard to ever follow through.

Karmann Ghias are notorious for the way their floors rot away from the road salt that municipalities use to de-ice the streets. The floor can disappear completely over the years, as was the case with my vehicle. I had to use a single lead pipe running across the frame to keep my car seat from falling into the street. When the cop came to my rolled-down window, I could hear his chortle immediately. As I tried to explain the situation, his laugh grew to something a little steadier, and eventually morphed into wheezing, with an occasional need to bend forward and hold his knee for support.

Without a floorboard, the snow I'd been driving through had been kicked up by my left front tire, and a continuous powerful jet spray had been hitting my chest. Down every street I had been subjected to the equivalent of a winter sandblasting. Meanwhile, the right front tire had been doing the same thing to the empty passenger seat beside me, burying it in a mound of gray-white slush. By the time I'd been pulled over, the interior was filled like a cream donut, and I had only my head and shoulders visible above it. That's how the officer found me at the wheel, and the free entertainment took the place of a $90 fine on that blustery afternoon. He thanked me for the show, and before leaving he snapped a photo to pass along to his sergeant.

Laughing at the failings and folly of others works as a seasonal stress reliever. I have neighbors who are elderly and retired, and like so many older folks, they find joy in the simple things, like a warm fire in the fireplace, or a good book, or a cup of hot coffee enhanced with a few drops of Irish whiskey in the late afternoon. If pressed, they'll tell you they have one guilty pleasure on those slow winter days, a pleasure that often accompanies those Irish coffees. While they're not proud of their pastime, it's a relatively innocuous hobby and it's available to most everyone. The pair like to watch cars try to make it up the hill in front of their house on snowy days. Without four-wheel drive that hill leading up and out of the neighborhood is difficult to traverse. Some cars make it a quarter of the way, some half, and a select few go three-fourths of the way or better, wheels spinning furiously, yet never quite reaching the crest.

This is not the retired couple's only guilty pleasure, however. They also enjoy watching cars come the other way. There are several winter afternoons when the road becomes so slick that drivers coming down the hill lose the ability to steer their vehicles and they go into an uncontrollable spin. The grade is not steep enough for the slide to be deadly; it's more of a slow-motion loss of control, a sliding and spinning that happens in a gradual and theatrical way, resulting in many cars half-buried in snowbanks at the bottom, or, worst case, taking out the stop sign. Neighbors who know this is coming keep their cars off the street on such days. But sometimes a work truck or delivery van is parked along the way, and the afternoon turns into more of a demolition derby. No one is ever hurt, but the retirees still feel guilty about how much they enjoy sipping their mugs and watching the chaos from their window perch. They tell me this pastime alone keeps them from joining the meek gray-haired hordes escaping to Miami, where there isn't a fraction of the entertainment.

Everyone growing up in the North Country has been in a winter car accident. If they haven't, they're not trying hard enough. Sliding down the street with your steering wheel doing very little and your brakes doing even less is an inevitable adventure for a Northlander. If you've never experienced that thrill then the guy behind you has, and you've felt his how-do-you-do in the form of sudden whiplash.

Oh, we like to brag about our winter driving skills, and they do far surpass those of the Southern crowd, but we all had to learn from scratch. No one getting their license for the first time had it mastered. It takes a few years to become a winter driving pro, and on your way, you hit things, sometimes a lot of things.

My favorite part of the winter car accident is the way it differs wildly from the car accidents down South. So many winter collisions occur with plenty of time to think. Your average wreck in New Orleans happens suddenly. Something goes wrong in an instant, and you don't even know the accident is probable until it's already in the past. But in the North, you can find yourself hitting an icy stretch of roadway and heading into a slide that's reasonably slow and steady. Up ahead 40 feet there's a car stopped at a red light. That distance alone would prevent any accident on an afternoon drive through L.A. But here that distance doesn't mean a thing. That car at the light will get hit and you know it, and you have some time to ponder this impending accident. Sure, you're praying for a miracle, but you've been in this situation before and you know how it ends. At the last second that guy will look in his rear-view mirror, see the panic in your eyes, and make a desperate but fruitless move to the right, hoping you'll slide past him and T-bone the cross traffic instead. It's a selfish act on his part, but, c'mon, he has a BMW, and he just washed it. Of course, he's kidding himself if he thinks that little move is going to change the outcome. Too little too late. You're headed for him like a torpedo, and his big boat is taking as long to get out of the way as the USS Indianapolis. Meanwhile the laughter of that Greek god is echoing down the avenue, and you're still sliding, taking the opportunity to carefully mull over your car insurance plan while rearranging the day's agenda to make room for the consequences of an accident that has yet to occur. When it does, it's almost a relief to get it over with. And how angry can the guy in front of you be? He went through the same icy patch moments ago and only avoided an accident because there didn't happen to be a car in front of him.

He can act all superior if he wants to, but karma tends to take care of folks who go that route. All you need to do is get out of the car, apologize, and ask if he's all right. Then turn to the right and left and bow. Even if you can't see him or her, there's someone who's been spending the afternoon enjoying the free entertainment from a window perch, probably with an Irish coffee.

Cold

*"To appreciate the beauty of a snowflake, it is necessary to
stand in the cold."*
— **Aristotle**

Cold is a fierce, demanding presence. It's alive, it's in your face, and it
calls the shots. It can be an elder, it can be a mentor, it can be a brat,
but it's the boss. Step outside, and walk into its grip. Some days it will
move in for a hearty hug, some days an assault.

I have come to understand its moods. I studied it, even as a little
boy. I was left alone with it often and had to learn how to make
friends with it. In my family, we were sent outdoors in the winter the
same as summer. Mom wanted us out of the house. Sometimes there
were other kids to play with, sometimes there weren't. As a kid, I had
to learn which cold was fun, which cold was annoying, which cold
was painful, and which cold was dangerous. I came to understand it.
Over the years, I learned it wasn't a tyrant. It was a tutor. And I came
to admire those who allowed the cold to teach them, those who lived
their lives with the cold as their partner.

"Professor Popsicle" is one example. He can be found at the
University of Manitoba in Winnipeg, Canada. His real name is Dr.
Gordon Giesbrecht, but a man who engages in the type of activities
Giesbrecht does begs for a nickname.

He routinely hurls his body into partially frozen lakes,
intentionally breaks through the ice, and forces himself to save his

own life, with rescuers standing by in case he's too slow. Using a snowmobile or cross-country skis, he purposely moves beyond the safety of solid ice and out into open water, all in the name of research.

"I try to learn what happens to the body in such conditions," he told me, "so people dealing with this in a real crisis can be prepared."

Watching Canadians interact with the cold is akin to watching penguins engage with it. Canada and cold have a deeply intimate relationship. The word should be on their currency: "In cold we trust." Professor Popsicle trusts it, or at least he trusts how he deals with it.

"If you don't panic when you first fall through the ice, you have a real good shot at surviving," he said. "Most people hit the water, involuntarily hyperventilate, and then panic, gasping for air. In so doing, they swallow large amounts of water and it's over almost before it starts."

I have long been baffled by the number of stories I've read each year of people falling through the ice, in both the early part of the season and just before the spring thaw. I don't know if these wayward wanderers fail to read the same news stories I do, but after a few years of such reports it ought to be ingrained in a Northerner that putting faith in an early or late-season body of frozen water is a fool's game. A wise man trusts ice only in the heart of winter, and leaves the book ends to people like Giesbrecht.

If people disregard this sound advice, however, and find themselves no longer standing on a lake, but swimming in one, Professor Popsicle has learned the hard way what steps need to be taken.

"In the first minute, the body involuntarily hyperventilates," Giesbrecht told me. "It's called the 'Cold Shock Response.' There's nothing you can do about it. You'll have uncontrollable gasping for 60 seconds. During this period the most important thing is to just keep your head above water. Just concentrate on that."

Giesbrecht said that if you understand that hyperventilation is simply the natural response of the body, you won't panic. He said we should realize the body is doing what it's built to do. This involuntary response will pass after one minute, and it's critical, at that point, to remain calm. There's good reason to; you have time. There are several minutes available to you to pull yourself out of the water, and if you kick with your legs and pull your body forward with your arms, you can end up back on top of the ice, flat on your belly. There is no other way you want to get out, Giesbrecht said. Staying on your belly is the key. You want to spread out your weight. But before getting out of the water, make sure you're getting out in the direction you fell in. There was solid ice there just before that fall, so you want to pull yourself in that same direction. Once you have kicked your legs and propelled your body so your belly is up on the ice, Giesbrecht told me you need to stay flat and roll your body to that safer, firmer ice you were once walking, riding, or skiing on. Only after you're certain you've rolled far enough, do you then stand up. But here's the rub. Some people, weighted down with heavy clothing, make several failed attempts to escape and quickly loose muscle control.

"You have, at most, ten minutes to get out of that water before you will no longer be able to use your muscles. Your arms and legs will become useless. That's why it's important not to waste your time on ineffective approaches. The common mistake people make is trying to pull themselves straight up with their arms. Kicking your legs and staying as flat as you possibly can is the best way to move your body up onto the ice. And staying flat makes it less likely that you'll fall through again."

If those ten minutes do pass and you're not out, Giesbrecht said, you need to move to plan B. It's a frightening plan to rely on, but it beats the alternative. With your muscles no longer able to bail you out, you're now going to have to rely on being rescued by someone else. If you were out that day by yourself, that could mean a long wait. The good news is, once again, you have time.

"People are often surprised by how long you can stay in that icy water before dying of hypothermia. If you can keep yourself from drowning you have a solid hour, sometimes more. The key is to make it so even if your body were to slip into unconsciousness you remain above the water."

For that, Giesbrecht told me, it's best to lay your arms flat across the ice and have as much of your body out of the water as possible. You remain very still and allow your arms to freeze to the ice sheet. It's like gluing yourself in place. You're creating conditions that will allow you to keep from drowning even if you fall into unconsciousness. People have been found in this state and have been rescued, sometimes with just their beard frozen to the ice, keeping their head from slipping beneath the surface.

There is, of course, another effective way to stay alive, and it'll be mentioned by residents of warmer climates: Move. But that's a word that's also been directed at those who live with deadly heat or hurricanes or floods or forest fires. No climate comes without trade-offs. It comes down to what trade-offs a person is willing to make.

Having spent a year living where winter is nonexistent and summer is a cauldron, I know the trade-offs I'm willing to make. I think it first hit me on a scorcher of a summer afternoon in the American South. When I looked out the window at the summer scenery, it looked as pretty as any day the Earth had ever offered. I saw long, lush lawns and rich, green leaves lit by the intense sunshine, and above it all the sweetest blue sky I'd ever encountered. I heard songbirds filling the air with exquisite music. It enticed, it lured, it seduced. But, when I stepped outside, I realized it was a ruse. I was ambushed. The oppressive heat and humidity descended like a sledgehammer. Hell had come to earth. I'd been bamboozled by beauty.

We all learn, growing up, what a perfect day looks like, and through the window, this one had it all. Yet I spent the rest of that day cooped up in artificial air conditioning, feeling the strangest and most awkward sense of cognitive dissonance. Every fiber in my body urged me to go revel in that glorious scene out the window. Yet I knew no pleasure waited there. One can only take off so much clothing, and even if I were naked that furnace would have been unbearable. The world didn't make sense to me that afternoon.

But flip the script, and there's not the same lament. When summer is over in the North and fall passes, winter offers its own window scenes. But those scenes are not deceptive. There is no trickster at work cajoling us with the promise of ideal outdoor conditions. It looks from inside the way it will feel on the outside. Icicles and bare tree branches covered in snow send a clear message. Inside, there are people sitting around the hearth, watching the warming fire and sipping hot drinks. Some Hollywood director stumbling upon this scene would find it harmonious, even iconic, a warm inviting interior world accented by a snowy vista through a picture window. Show me an idyllic, made-for-the-big-screen scene where the family huddles around the droning hum of some cold gray air conditioner, as the forbidding imagery out the window appears as paradise. As they say in Alabama, "That dog don't hunt."

So, I choose the cold North, where I can trust the scene out my window. And when that scene appears frosty, I can still find good reason to head out and frolic, mostly due to a man from the Netherlands who has preached to the world the almost sacred healing power of the cold. There is nothing that has made me happier to live in a Northern climate than to have encountered the force of nature known as "Wim Hof." In modern times, no one person has done more to rehabilitate the word "cold."

We can all agree that no one longs to be treated in a cold manner. We don't appreciate the cold shoulder. No one wants cold water thrown on their plans. The word "cold" has gotten a bad rap. So, it's startling to listen to Wim Hof, a man with a reverence for cold that would shock even the heartiest Northerner.

"The cold is a noble force," he argues. "The cold is a warm friend whom I hold dear. The cold is a doorway to the soul. The cold is my god."

It's not hyperbole. Few people on Earth have spent more time purposely immersing themselves in cold conditions that seem antithetical to healthy living. Swimming in icy water, rolling around in snow in nothing but shorts, burying himself to the neck in heaps of ice are all different ways Wim Hof says he stays well physically, mentally, and emotionally. This human curiosity, nicknamed "Ice Man," has come to view cold as a leading player in bringing vitality, strength, and happiness to humanity. As scientists study his claims and find many of them credible, he is radically altering the view of a cold winter day. Those subfreezing temperatures are our friends, Wim Hof argues. Go out and spend time with them. Your body will benefit from the experience.

Thanks in part to Wim Hof, there's now scientific evidence that exposure to the cold contributes to good health and well-being by stimulating metabolism, thus reducing inflammation, relieving depression, and strengthening the cardiovascular system.

Nevertheless, investigative journalist Scott Carney once thought Wim Hof needed to be taken down a peg, that his health claims were quack chicanery.

Carney watched social media videos of the Ice Man climbing snowy mountains in shorts, swimming blithely under the ice sheet of a frozen lake, and telling all who'd listen that cold is beautiful. Carney just couldn't stomach it. He booked a flight to Wim Hof's training facility in Poland, where he teaches all comers how to do exactly what he does, telling them it's no trick, that they too can take control of their bodies' autonomic processes such as their immune system and metabolism and access superhuman powers of endurance and strength.

Carney told me he was intending to return to the United States having exposed "this nonsense" for what it was. Instead, he gave the world the New York Times best-seller, "What Doesn't Kill Us," a book confirming much of what Wim Hof promotes.

Carney said he went from a guy living in perpetually warm Los Angeles to relaxing comfortably in shorts in 2-degree weather in just a matter of days. He soon gained stamina, lost fat, grew healthier and stronger, and became an ardent fan of this aging, energetic Dutchman with the youthful zest for life and the contagious enthusiasm for passing along all he's learned from his beloved cold.

Wim Hof combines deep-breathing exercises with cold immersion and says it's that critical one-two punch that serves the body so well. It has allowed him to control his immune system, he says, as well as his autonomic nervous system. When scientists told him this wasn't possible, Wim Hof offered to train them and to deliver the very same results. Like Carney, the scientists took him up on it and were soon stunned. The following appeared, afterward, in the prestigious medical journal *Proceedings of the National Academy of Sciences* (PNAS):

"Hitherto, both the autonomic nervous system and innate immune system were regarded as systems that cannot be voluntarily influenced. The present study demonstrates that, through practicing techniques learned in a short-term training program, the sympathetic nervous system and immune system can indeed be voluntarily influenced."

Carney said, in his investigative work, he came to see that most of Western civilization lives in a state of perpetual homeostasis, constantly seeking and finding that comfortable room temperature of roughly 70 degrees. But we're built, he said, to endure great fluctuations in temperature, and our sympathetic and parasympathetic nervous systems are designed to manage these fluctuations. We don't give them that task anymore, he says, and our health suffers because of it.

"Everyone likes the warmth," Carney said. "Everyone enjoys curling up by a nice fire and coming into the safety of their home. But what the cold offers us is contrast, which we don't get enough of as humans. Most of us seek for our bodies a kind perpetual state of summer."

Carney said that what he realized researching Wim Hof's work is that the modern world has made it too easy to find that comfortable 70-degree temp most everywhere we go. It's being manufactured for us in different environments, from our cars to our indoor stadiums and shopping malls, and it's doing our health a disservice.

"Our biology is primed to take on the seasons," Carney said. "Cold exercises parts of our nervous system and exercises our circulatory system. We hear constantly about the two great pillars of health: diet and exercise. But what we're learning is there's a third. The environment. Giving your body contrasting environments offers it the opportunity to do what it's designed to do."

Carney said Wim Hof's students are systematically training their bodies by taking on the hardship of cold, sure as one trains the body by taking on the struggle of vigorous exercise. And because he believes human beings are suffering for lack of exposure to environmental extremes, he's created a social media campaign called "wear one less layer." The idea, he said, is to feel a little chilly.

"We've just become too weak and anti-resilient, and it's time to change that by getting back in touch with the cold."

Urban Impound Lot

"While I relish our warm months, winter forms our character."
— **Tom Allen, Congressman from Maine**

If you've had a car towed to an impound lot because you left it out on the street after a "snow emergency" was declared, you have a vague sense of what it must feel like to be at the mercy of kidnappers. A car that you own outright is now in the hands of strangers who are charging you for the right to drive it home. Until you pay up, it's locked in a prison yard and will remain there, with the high cost of retrieving it growing by the day.

How much do you really love your car? Enough to free it from a drab and gritty corner of the city, surrounded by high fencing and guarded by morose workers who have grown callous from years of dealing with aggrieved citizens?

Many new arrivals to the North are certain their vehicle has been stolen. The shock of seeing an empty space where it once was parked takes time to absorb. "I swear it was right here just last night," they'll exclaim, wide-eyed. And it surely was. Soon, empathetic neighbors will pass along the bad news. "You left it on the street? Oh, buddy, I'm so sorry. The city was towing last night."

Those words land with a sickening thud, followed by an audible sigh. From now until that car is back in your possession, life will be a bureaucratic migraine. You've not only been towed but also ticketed.

You'll need to pay the ticket and the towing fee, show updated insurance information, and of course you'll need someone to drive you to that forlorn and forgotten part of the city, to a lot that resembles a Soviet Eastern Bloc detention center. There you will find your place behind an agonizingly long line of irritated and despondent people who are paying money they don't have to purchase a vehicle they already own.

Elsewhere in the city, however, there are contented snowplow drivers turning down residential streets with their plows scraping loudly against the frozen ground. As far as their eyes can see, the street is clear of obstructions. They have a nice, clean line that the plow can hug, and it follows the curb block after block.

There is something uniquely beautiful about a perfectly plowed street bordered by giant mounds of white snow covering the boulevards, yards, and sidewalks. It's akin to a ray of sunlight shining down a dark forest path. There's suddenly a way out. The cars that will back out of driveways will easily drive away from this neighborhood, and those returning will find ample access straight to their front door. It's one of the first signs of civilization after a blizzard. A man-made machine turns a corner and opens an arterial route through a clustered community. It's a neighborhood's first counterpunch to the haymaker of a big snowfall. It's the taming of winter, a sign that a city will be working alongside this formidable season, not working against it.

The plow drivers who come down a street with buried cars mucking up their clean plow-lines must cuss under their breath. They want to take pride in their work. They prefer to stare at their efforts in their rear-view mirror and see an unblemished path. Those snow-covered cars are anathema. I figure they tow them away in their minds just to pass the time, recklessly yanking them at high speeds, taking corners too tightly, allowing the vehicles to scrape violently against stop signs and ram into lampposts.

Most Northerners eventually learn the natural order of things. They learn that significant snowfall brings plows and tow trucks. They determine whether they live on a night plow route or a day plow route, or if they have an even side of the street address or an odd side, whatever criteria a municipality is using. They memorize it sure as they do "spring forward and fall back" for daylight saving time. It becomes ingrained, and their car is never towed again, and their street is cleared curb to curb flawlessly, and everyone is happy. But that's taking responsibility, and that's growing up, and that takes time, and there will be wakeup calls along the road to full-fledged Northern maturity.

A suggestion: Bring the staff at the impound lot some homemade cookies. They have a tough job and few are kind to them. They work in a studio back lot re-creation of Bulgaria circa 1957, and they never imagined this life for themselves when they first saw a cop as a young kid and thought being a civil servant would be rewarding. Who knows who they angered or insulted, resulting in this assignment. They're stuck here now, and they could use some compassion. So, offer them some and they just might send it back your way. If you get a smile out of them, tell the world. You'll be the first.

Winter Window #3

In the tender glow
from the streetlight
the delicate frost on my window
mimics intricate stained glass

disguising its role as a solider

I ponder the polarities
The cocoon of my bed
this winter womb
beside dagger-cold air
marauding outdoors

In the hours before dawn
no gold or silver
will buy a kinder world
than that offered by this crystal castle
framed in drapes

a luminous sentry
separating life from death

Winter's Shadow Side

"Blow, blow, thou winter wind, thou art not so unkind as man's ingratitude."
— **William Shakespeare**

Standing near the front door of our neighborhood hardware store, Herman Crull is in fine form: "Behind my back these wise-ass neighbor kids call me 'Cranky Crull.' They don't think I know, but I know. They snicker and sneer and act as if they're never going to arrive at old age. But I tell 'em all, 'You just wait!'"

I take advantage of a pause in the conversation to mention that my friend is waiting in the car, but Herman isn't listening. He's telling me that "being ornery" is merely the byproduct of accumulated annoyances and that winter is the greatest annoyance of them all.

"My wife says I'm in a bad mood December to March," Herman says. "Well, guess what? Nature is in a bad mood December to March. I'm just tagging along."

There is a caustic charm to Herman, but its appeal doesn't reveal itself easily. Nevertheless, anyone who drifts into caricature as comfortably as he does can't be taken too seriously.

"I tell you, this North Country is not a place where people were supposed to live permanently. They were supposed to visit, then get out. The message didn't get through, or it got mistranslated, or it fell into the hands of the illiterate, or the first to migrate here were kicked in the head by a mule. The judgment centers in the frontal lobes were shorting out."

In his thick wool shirt and work boots, Herman presents like a North Country logo. He is as emblematic as the stoic farm couple in Grant Wood's "American Gothic." His face is angular, his nose thin and pointy, and the only hair on his head rests around his ears, like a car's quarter panels framing its wheels.

"There are places on earth that we all seem to agree no one should inhabit. There are inhospitable deserts and vast ice sheets that are accepted as 'no man's lands.' There are thick tropical jungles filled with an endless variety of biting insects and wretched snakes and other despicable creatures no one was ever supposed to encounter. We all have made peace with leaving parts of this earth to lower life forms and to the elements. What the hell happened here?"

Though Herman's musings can be comical, he never smiles while delivering them. Those of us who've spent time with him have come to view this venting as therapeutic for the old fella. And beneath the exaggeration, it's heartfelt. Herman falls into the category of those who despise winter. He stays here only because his wife won't leave, and she won't leave only because their four grandchildren live here. Herman feels trapped, and it eats away at him.

"You ever see an old person go for a walk in the winter? This neighbor's sidewalk is shoveled, but this next guy's walkway is an ice sheet, and the guy after that has a one-foot snow path, and the one after that shoveled half of his walk and gave up. It's hopeless. So, we all stay home. Do those folks know one fall could do us in? Do they care?"

Herman is not alone in his distress and dismay. And he can find kindred spirits at all ages. You can hear it in a cafe when a young couple walks in from a numbing winter wind, and one says to the other, "Good lord, why do we live here?"

Therese Nilsson is 29 and ready to join the Herman Crull Club. It's mid-February, and she's already had her fill.

"There are days when the sky is a gray and the snow has grown dull and the street is slushy and the trees are lifeless, and in all directions, it just looks blah," Therese tells me. "I get so depressed. I look at the calendar and see there's still six weeks left in the season. A panic sets in. I realize I must get out. I have to buy an airline ticket south, just to feel a warm sun and see some blue water. I think the absence of color does me in, it takes me down. I need to see rich hues once again just to feel alive."

It's known as the shadow side of winter, and it's every bit as real as winter's grace and beauty. In its own strange way, it's the greatest teacher of all, because it shows how one's perspective, approach, and attitude radically alter one's daily experience. It drives home the message that how we receive life will pivot on our disposition and outlook.

David and Denise Ramirez should never have moved North. He accepted a job transfer, and they made the long trek from Valdosta, Georgia, over a long weekend in late September.

"We visited one time in early July and loved it," Denise says. "But by mid-November we were already getting a little worried.

"Neither of us were prepared. We were told this wasn't anywhere near winter yet. When the snow came, we had no idea how to drive in it. We both had car accidents immediately. By mid-December, we were experiencing temperatures we had only felt one or two times in our entire lives. On several weekends, we just refused to leave the house, until we realized a person can't go on living this way and stay sane."

By late January, David was talking to his company about taking a pay cut and moving back to Valdosta. Denise was asking neighbors for advice, unsure of how she was going to get through two more months of this.

"They were all so calm and happy, these people," Denise says. "They laughed and joked about it, but it wasn't funny to me. I tried to follow their advice for how to dress and enjoy myself outdoors, comfortably, but all I wanted to do was stay in, turn up the heat, and cook. I gained more weight that winter than I ever have in my life."

When one has lived one's entire existence in the North, it's difficult to view it through a transplant's eyes. It's startling the first time you're around someone who is shivering uncontrollably on a windless day with relatively mild temps in the low 20s. You worry how they're going to function when it really gets cold.

Paul Decker didn't come from a warm climate. He moved up from Nebraska. But he says he didn't much care for the winters there either. When he hit the Northland, however, he says winter morphed into a parade of headaches.

"I've been here five years now, and all I think about in winter is how aggravating everything is. Cold is aggravating, period. The car door gets frozen shut, or the car door opens but the car windows are frozen shut. I have a poorly insulated house, and when the temps dip under 10 below I have to run the faucets all night or I lose my running water. I had a huge icicle fall from the gutter last week and careen into a window, cracking it. I went out to heat up my car two months ago and, while it was warming up, I went back into the house. My plan was to wait a bit so as to be able to relax with my morning coffee in a warm car as I drove to work and not have to wait miles for the vehicle to become acceptable for human habitation. But I guess one can't do that anymore. My car was stolen. I couldn't have made it any easier for the crook. I'm sure he was delighted by the pleasant temp, as he drove off listening to my favorite radio station."

There is a point where this complaining can get tedious. One wonders if these people have come to expect more comfort and good times from life than life was ever intended to deliver with consistency.

Many a sultry, steamy summer night can make sleeping impossible, but few can claim to have trouble getting warm under wool blankets on a winter night. Many a summer thunderstorm has ruined an outdoor picnic, ball game, or day at the beach, but rarely does a snowfall ruin anyone's fun. You see people skiing in the snow, sliding in the snow, ice fishing in the snow, taking walks in the snow. In fact, a snowfall can often enhance an afternoon.

Life can hit you with spitballs on any given day in a host of different ways. Winter is not worth blaming for one's mood.

The crime rate is higher in warm weather. Frigid days have a way of dampening one's enthusiasm for lawlessness. Summer comes with flies, gnats, mosquitoes, and disease-carrying ticks. Winter sends them packing, and the clear air becomes free of those annoying visitors. In fact, the air itself is cleaner in the winter. Snowfalls pull pollutants from the air. There is no finer time to go out and breathe in the outdoors than after a snowfall.

No, it just isn't possible that one season can be the culprit behind all the woes of these complainers. But then again, winter is a season my body was built for. We're all made differently. I do have sympathy for those who struggle. One should live where climate and soul are in sync. My advice to these people is to open that big national map and find a world where happiness waits.

"You know where you can stick that map?" Herman asks me, spitting the words this time. "There's such a thing as being trapped, mister. And you're looking at it. I've got a brother in San Bernardino who says he has a nice duplex waiting if I can talk my wife into leaving. Well, all that amounts to is a tease, 'cuz she ain't going anywhere. In fact, she's at the rink right now, laughing and watching the grandkids skate. So, you can fold that map six ways and put it where the moon don't shine."

The Artist in Winter

"I write probably 80 percent of my songs over the winter."
— **Bob Seger, lifelong Michigan resident**

Whenever I visit with Northern artists, I'm routinely enchanted by the unique perspective they bring to our shared world. No matter the medium they work in, their frame of reference often brings a revelation that's refreshing and capable of shifting the way I see things. Such is the case when talking to them about winter. They can reveal the season's power in unexpected ways.

For instance, poet Isadora Gruye told me, "Winter in the North is a spooky time of year, in my view. People think of Halloween and October as the spooky time, but I see Halloween as just the kick-off to an entire spooky season. Let's face it, winter is a little creepy. It's ghostlike. You go outside and the land seems haunted. It's desolate. It's the season that's used as the metaphor for death, after all. Even the sounds seem haunted. The wind doesn't gently rustle the leaves, it howls through dead branches."

Paradoxically, Isadora said, winter is the season when she feels "most fiercely alive."

"The elements all seem to be working against us. And I get revved up by that. You hear people talk about slowing down or hibernating, but I get energized. I adopt this attitude that says, you're not going to win, you're not going to beat me."

Novelist Will Weaver told me he writes with the seasons, and they dictate his pace. Winter is not only the time to turn up the heat in his home, he said, but in his work as well.

"A good hard Northern winter is a writer's best friend. It sometimes takes something dramatic to keep us in our chair, to keep us working, to keep us focused. I have a hard time sticking with a novel in the warm weather. Too many other things I like to do."

Will spoke of the way winter fuels his work more by what it removes from the landscape than what it adds. He compared a winter vista to a sheet of typing paper and said the emptiness allows his imagination to fill the void.

"There's something about a winter field or a frozen lake that's the equivalent of that blank white page. You look out your window and it's up to you to fill in that vast space, as a writer, or as an artist."

Will's metaphor of a snow-covered field or ice-covered lake as a blank page or empty canvas highlights something I've long sensed but until now have not been able to articulate. The idea that the land growing sparse, winnowed down to vast white fields and stark bare branches, frees the mind to get busy filling the emptiness. What is taken away leaves us with opportunity. As nature removes color, texture, and variety from our surroundings, it allows the foliage of our imagination to grow lush. We balance the scales by working the soil of our minds, our hearts, and our souls. An interior landscape blossoms.

The northern states of the central U.S. are colder than elsewhere in the country, and the northern boundaries of those states are the coldest of the cold, but that's exactly where Tim Stouffer, writer, painter, and photographer, wanted to raise a family. He's not a native of the North. When he left Illinois as an adult, he said he could have moved south, east, or west. He chose instead, Ely, Minnesota, the last populated town before entering Canada. It was 35-below zero on the day I spoke with him.

"I like to go winter camping," Tim said. "And up here you can easily camp right on the middle of a frozen lake. There is nothing else in the world quite like lying on the hard ice in the dark and waking up to the sound of it expanding or contracting beneath you as the temperatures change throughout the night."

The sheet of ice on a lake is like the skin of a drum. It's a membrane that allows sound created on one end of a great expanse to easily be heard on the far end. Haunting groans, moans, twangs, pops, and pings can echo in the darkness. Tim told me these sounds will fill the air and create seemingly otherworldly moments that no one who hasn't experienced them could ever fully appreciate or understand. To know that mysterious, evocative sound, however, one must make a certain peace with the deep cold.

"I like the cold," Tim told me. "I like how it makes you feel, how it makes you think, and what you experience being in it. I compare it to being out at night in the dark. A lot of people don't particularly care for the darkness, but that, too, has always been appealing to me, even when I was a kid. Growing up in Illinois, I liked to go into the woods at night and be under the stars. Just to experience it. Not to do anything necessarily, just to be. Being out in the cold brings up things that I then want to write about. It brings up things I want to think about. You just experience everything in a new way. It's a very different world. And different in a way that a really hot summer day is not all that different."

Tim said there's a "thrill" to the cold, an excitement to it. He said the people where he lives get more animated when the arctic air arrives.

"You can feel the people get charged up up here. They have to talk about it. They want to share stories of what they experienced. The cold here calls attention to itself in a way it doesn't where there are milder winters."

Speaking with Tim, one gets an image of the cold as a domineering personality, an alive and lively member of the community with whom every man, woman, and child has an intimate relationship. And if that relationship can, at times, bring painful struggle, Tim said there's something appealing about that as well.

"There aren't a lot of places left in the country where survival is an aspect of life. That's been removed from much of our existence. But if you're going to spend time outdoors here, you have to build up a fair amount of knowledge and understanding of how to deal with the elements. If you're going out dog sledding or ice fishing or winter camping, you could easily be dealing with 30 below and there's a lot to know about being out in that. And there's a certain amount of pride that people take up here in their understanding of what it takes to engage with this cold."

Visiting with Tim, I came to ponder the notion that perhaps much of life has become too tame, too easy, and no longer calls on any of our ancient skills for successfully combating the elements. Few long for a truly primitive era, but maybe much of the industrial world has moved too far in the other direction, and what Tim has come to embrace is a deep human need to occasionally be confronted by one's surroundings, not always comforted by them. In fact, it's safe to say few artists do any of their best work when most at ease and least challenged.

Painter Nancy Ensley also believes there is something in interacting with the cold that focuses the mind on the essentials of living and wakes up a part of the soul that can fall asleep in a world of comfort. Her deep woods cabin, also near the Canadian border, is a long way from the life she knew growing up in the state of Virginia.

"As a young girl, I remember being fascinated with the North," she says. "That's where I wanted to go. I'd look at a map and be intrigued by Minnesota or by Alaska. Places that had extreme cold."

Nancy said when she eventually moved north, she would hear visitors argue that "when the temperature drops below zero there's no sense parsing out the degrees anymore. It's all the same at that point. It's just plain cold." But she found that wasn't true at all.

"Up here, you come to see the real differences between a 10 degree below zero day and a 20 below zero day, and how it's not at all like a 30 degree below zero day, and how different still 40 below zero is. People understand 10 degree swings and what they mean in the summer, but it's fascinating to experience those differences in the deep cold."

Nancy paints the wildlife and the wilderness around her, entranced by the different kinds of beauty one encounters in winter. She reminded me of one of the most enjoyable offerings of any evening snowfall: The ability to wake the next morning and encounter a varied array of winding, intersecting tracks detailing the busy life of the nocturnal animal world. Creatures who would leave few tell-tale signs of their presence on an autumn or spring night leave an entire story in that fresh morning snow. "Suddenly you're made aware of all the activity going on outside your door while you're sleeping," she said.

I had heard another man years ago describe this as the script of a play left on his doorstep on winter mornings. He told me that, as he studied the script, the choreography of the night before would come to life in his mind. He would move through those hours in his imagination, seeing all the different animals moving purposefully and unchallenged, freed from concerns of human contact.

Artist Neil Sherman said, for a landscape painter, a Northern winter is the time one can finally "see through things." He told me a summertime vista is "filled in with thick, flourishing life and does not offer the depth of perspective that appears when so much of that life is stripped bare." He said there's no landscape subject for his paintbrush that changes as dramatically as the wilderness of summer viewed again six months later.

Neil told me winter has an appealing way of removing the evidence of any human interaction with the environment, as if the season were reclaiming the land.

"One of my favorite things to do, in the winter, is to travel to someplace in the woods, maybe to a small river, where you have to use snowshoes to get there, and then to realize, looking around, that no one else has been there, at least not recently, because there isn't a single footprint in any direction. Your tracks are the first tracks to appear."

In discovering such places, Neil said, he's captivated by the way winter can make the world feel brand new. He said he can't get the same sensation hiking on a wilderness trail in the summer. There's no evidence that on this day he alone has come to this spot.

"I live near Lake Superior, and another thing I really like about winter, as a painter, is the way steam will come off that lake when it gets below zero. It's a phenomenon few people in the world get to experience. I've painted it numerous times."

The phenomenon Neil referred to is often called "sea smoke." The relatively warmer lake water sends billowing clouds into the much cooler air. If this is accompanied by strong winds from the north, "sea devils" can sometimes form, appearing as eerie, smoky twisters mixing with the mist above the water. What painter, with an easel, could resist such a unique and ghostly spectacle?

Artist Andy Messerschmidt also chose the Canadian border for his home and compares winter there to a "psychedelic drug trip." Like such an experience, he said, the pleasurable, the bewildering, and the terrifying can all present themselves to the psyche at different times, depending on conditions and circumstances.

"What I mean when I compare it to a drug experience is that, when the winter starts, I say to myself, yeah, I can handle this weirdness, I've dealt with this before. And then I go deeper and deeper into the season and it gets colder and colder and more intense, and I start to get these panicky sensations, like one might on some psychedelic drug trip, as everything gets to be almost too much. You hear of these metaphysical explorers in different cultures who take these substances and encounter all these strange and sometimes disturbing worlds. But if they do it often enough, they come to no longer be afraid of what they know they'll encounter. Where I live, up here on the border, the cold is the most extreme of anywhere else in the country, and when it really starts to kick in in January, I say to myself, oh man, am I ready for this again?"

Like other artists, Andy said winter is an extraordinarily productive time for him. He's most prolific from December through March. But he does not burrow into his art studio and turn his back on the cold. He embraces all that the outdoors has to offer. As an artist, he said he derives inspiration from the way winter routinely alters his frame of mind.

"I was on a frozen lake doing some fishing recently. I was there all day long. The sun wasn't out, the sky was gray, the snow was pure white, and the trees on shore offered no color whatsoever. Hours and hours in that environment. And then towards the end of the day a buddy of mine pulled up on a snowmobile. On the side of it was a single stripe of neon pink and a single stripe of neon green. And, I know this sounds weird, but I almost fell to my knees looking at that. It was just so powerfully vivid and so stunning, after all that gray and white. I'm serious when I say it was almost overwhelming."

There are artists who appreciate their winter surroundings, and then there are artists whose chosen medium is winter itself, specifically ice and snow. All over the Northland artists with chainsaws, handsaws, hairdryers, irons, chisels, and blow torches create remarkably intricate works of art out of snow and ice. Massive dragons, medieval warriors, and giant castles have been commonplace at winter festivals for decades.

But the creative use of winter's frozen offerings doesn't stop there. Artist Helen Chadwick was famous for inventing and selling a most unusual form of winter art. Her process involved urinating in the deep snow and then making casts of the interior spaces that had melted away from that warm liquid. The completed forms of bronze and cellulose lacquer have been described by art critics as "winter wonderlands" that appear as "alien cities from a frozen planet." Not surprisingly, Chadwick has received less enthusiastic critiques from many in the public who have found themselves repelled when encountering her creations at professional galleries. Regardless, she deserves credit for coming up with yet another creative use of snow, and one that once again has the bracing cold winter working to an artist's advantage. Her detractors would be flummoxed to learn that a single urine-designed sculpture by Chadwick sold for over $30,000.

Slip-Slide Sublime

"Welcome to winter. When fifty percent of drivers should have their licenses temporarily suspended."
— **Kelley Armstrong, author**

When I received my driver's license at 16, I approached winter with the eye of the tiger. Snow, ice, and an automobile were a thrilling combination for a youthful imagination. Back then, all my favorite cop shows featured a fishtailing vehicle rounding some corner in a frenzied car chase, something I could never hope to pull off on dry pavement, but a maneuver that was easily attainable on snowy streets.

On winter days, there was a deeply satisfying adrenaline rush when rounding a corner and having the back end of my car swerve, forcing me to overcorrect with the steering wheel, sending the back end swerving in the other direction. That simple, joyful fishtail movement was something I came to master and to create at will, whenever the streets were quiet, mostly at night. I took an otherwise simple turn and made it a poor man's joyride. My parents never knew about this, of course, or I wouldn't have been given the keys. But had they thought about it, they might have realized that, to a 16-year-old, a car is merely a larger version of a go-cart.

One could argue whether a driver's license should be handed to someone almost a decade away from a fully developed adult brain, but that discussion is for a different book. Suffice it to say, my finest winter memories from my teens are filled with irresponsible winter driving.

Intentional fishtailing on city streets was not the only joy I pursued with four wheels and wicked winter weather. My favorite cheap high was finding empty department store parking lots, hours after closing time. The snow and ice mix and the wide-open spaces allowed for speeding across the lot and then hitting the brakes hard, forcing the car to swerve, slide, and careen, as I howled with impish delight. Those poor kids in Southern California, I thought, they have no idea what they're missing.

Some of my friends had four-wheel drive vehicles, and that always upped the ante. Driving in the midst of a 14-inch snowfall, late at night, one practically had the city streets to oneself. The world outside the windshield was beautiful and chaotic and the vehicle was unstoppable. We'd seek out snowbanks just to blast through them, the powder exploding in all directions. And we'd always take time to play savior, stopping to pull a stuck vehicle from an otherwise hopeless situation, before tearing off into the night like superheroes.

Late night during a blizzard was an almost mystical time to be on the road. Foolhardy some would say, but a glorious free-for-all for fearless young men. The frenetic presentation of a winter storm perfectly matched the high-spirited independence of our youth. We felt as wild and free as the weather itself. Lane markers on all the roads vanished under the powder, sometimes even the border between roadways and boulevards. The land was returning to the wild pristine prairie of yesteryear, right before our eyes. Summer nights driving around the lakes with the windows down had its charms, of course, but winter driving was otherworldly. We were in a parallel universe, where the very laws of physics seemed to shift.

One cold, snowy night, there were four of us in the car driving down a freeway, having left our college dormitory, heading to a concert in the city. As we entered the outskirts of town with cars behind us and ahead of us, our vehicle began a spontaneous fishtail. This time, however, there was no effective steering wheel correction. The tail of the car just kept moving in one direction, bringing the front of the car, which had been traveling south, to a position now facing east, and then spinning it farther until it was pointing north, and it just kept going. We were doing a complete 360-degree spin in the middle of the road while traveling 50 miles per hour. On either side of us were ditches that would have brought an end to our evening plans. In front of us and behind us were vehicles we could have hit violently. But, before we could even scream, the car came full circle and pointed us south once more, the wheels rolling on, at that same 50 miles per hour clip. It had been nothing more than automobile ballet, highway ice follies. The car had chosen to gracefully perform a lutz, or is it an axel, in the midst of its long journey. And like the exhilaration a figure skater must feel, we four young men felt an ecstatic charge move through us as we roared with exuberant laughter that seemed to be a combination of incredulity, fear, and relief. One swift 360-spin, perfectly performed in the middle of the road at high speed, and it hadn't taken so much as seconds off our trip. No Hollywood stunt driver could have delivered this with greater finesse. We decided then and there that we had a magic car. Winter had brought out the showman in this rusty beater, and it performed under the bright white lights of those suburban roads like a circus act, offering everything but a closing bow.

Come spring, the fun would always end, and driving would once again become a civilized endeavor for responsible citizens. Cars would return to their well-behaved ways, and the world would become tediously predictable. But we had our stories, always, and we repeated them often when playful memories would send us tumbling back into those wild winters.

This Is Nothing

- a short story -

"If the weather were a person, it would be simultaneously the most popular and most bullied kid in school."
— **Stephen Kokx, author**

The marriage of Glen and Connie Comstock has been tested by winter season after season for 28 years. They're still together and resigned to their love, but they finally decided this year to sleep in separate bedrooms when winter pillow-talk grew contentious yet again. They also agreed to get their own separate cars, having learned the hard lesson that sharing was untenable due to their vastly different winter driving styles.

A few people in the town of Larsburg, North Dakota, secretly delight in listening to Glen and Connie's continual bickering. To them, the couple's squabbles are the whimsical soundtrack of small-town life. Others find it disturbing and will leave a cafe or bar shortly after seeing the pair walk in the front door.

Rita is Glen and Connie's oldest child. She graduated from high school, pursued salon training, and is now a hairdresser in Larsburg. She said weather is most often the springboard for her parents' disagreements.

"Mom's always been a worrier," Rita said. "When the snow starts falling hard, she's on her phone seeing where her kids are, telling us to stay off the roads. We're adults now, and we know how to handle it, but that doesn't seem to matter. If it gets down to double digits below zero, she goes a little crazy if she can't reach one of us. All winter she's checking the weather forecast and registering varying degrees of concern. Meanwhile, Dad is the complete opposite."

However difficult it might be to live with a chronic worrier, Rita says, it's no less annoying spending time with her dad. He refuses to view any inclement weather as cause for adjustment, no matter the severity, believing the harshness of winter is "all in the head." If Connie complains about bitter cold temperatures, Glen will pull out a favorite tale of someone who has suffered far worse and complained far less.

"You think Shackleton had a pity party?" he'll ask, referring to the British explorer Ernest Shackleton, who was trapped in the Arctic ice for a year with the sailing crew of the *Endurance*.

If Connie is seen driving cautiously after a heavy snowfall, Glen will laugh and ask if she's just arrived from Scottsdale.

"Seriously, honey, I have old college buddies in Buffalo who take out their sports cars in this kind of weather. This is nothing. If you know how to drive in snow, it shouldn't slow you a lick."

Rita says it was the same way when she and her brother were growing up.

"We got cold a lot. It gets painfully cold here in Larsburg, and Dad always wanted to do stuff outside. We'd be out with him, saying we couldn't stand it any longer, begging him to take us home, and he'd be describing a situation where someone survived conditions far deadlier."

"You know about 19-year-old Jean Hilliard, don't you?" he'd ask. "Her car broke down in 20 below weather back in 1980, and she walked two miles trying to find her way to the house of a friend. She collapsed on that person's doorstep and was found frozen the next morning with her eyes wide open. She was literally stiff as a board and had to be shoved into a car's back seat diagonally. At the hospital, her skin was too stiff to be punctured by a hypodermic needle. Her body temperature was too low to register on any thermometer. Her frozen eyes didn't respond to light. She looked like a corpse. But a few hours later she was warm and awake and talking with nurses like nothing had happened. Her only issue was some frostbite on the tips of her toes and fingers. I say if Jean could get through her ordeal, you kids can stick it out a bit longer."

Glen's cavalier attitude toward winter, combined with his wife's alarmist approach, make for fiery spectacles in the Comstock household. Rita described a visit recently where her mother was worrying that high winds would make the day seem far colder than the 10-degree forecast, and she and Glen should rethink their daily stroll, opting instead for the basement treadmill. Glen, unsurprisingly, would have none of it.

"It's above zero," Glen shouted. "You agreed we'd take our walks whenever it was above zero."

"Well, the wind chill means the 'feels-like' temp will be well below zero," Connie replied. "That's the temp I go by."

"The 'feels-like' temp?" Glen belted out, exasperated. "That's ridiculous. That's a subjective measurement that's going to vary from person to person. That's like asking if something is going to taste good or not. To whom?

"Wind chill is a made-up measurement for jacking the TV weather ratings," he continued. "Do you even know how they came up with wind chill? They had volunteers walk on a treadmill in a cold wind tunnel with sensors attached to the outside of their faces to take temperature readings, which they then used to calculate heat loss. That sounds like something out of a high school science fair. I think the time-honored mercury reading is the only thing we can go by, and that says we're walking."

But Connie was already in the basement, turning on the treadmill. The sound of its hum infuriated Glen, who yelled downstairs that Connie should go join her "friends in the wind tunnel" and live out her days like a "lab rat." Meanwhile, Glen said, he'd be "heading outdoors the way God intended."

Connie shot back that she hoped Glen ended up like Jean Hilliard. And if he did, he should know he's too fat to fit diagonally in her back seat.

"I never get involved in their arguments," Rita explained. "We kids learned long ago to just ignore them and get on with our lives. But it's hard when we're in public."

Rita said a gathering to celebrate her brother's 21st birthday was the latest example. The family met at Ida's Cafe on Main Street where Glen and Connie overheard diners at an adjacent booth complaining about ice dams on the roof of their house.

"Glen, are those ice dams on our house as well?" Connie asked. "Is that what's causing those huge icicles? I hate walking out the front door these days for fear one of them will break free and go right through my head. In fact, I think I'm using the back door from now on. Don't even ask me to get the mail. You need to do something about that."

Glen didn't know whether to glare at the folks at the next booth for bringing up the subject and dampening an upbeat birthday mood, or to chastise Connie for what he felt was her absurd anxiety over being impaled. He opted instead for what he considered a teachable moment involving his two grown children, both of whom were giving their mother some version of an eye roll.

"Kids, this is a way to live a life that you never want to emulate," Glen instructed. "The stress alone will shorten your life expectancy. Listen to what has your mother refusing to retrieve our mail from now on: Harmless icicles hanging decoratively from the eaves."

Then Glen returned to familiar territory, disjointed stories from the past.

"Back in 2010, Mike Edwards, the founding member of the Electric Light Orchestra, died when his van was hit by a 1,300-pound bale of hay that chose that particular moment while he was passing by to come rolling down a farm hill in England. There were maybe nine cars that day that drove down that road, and Mike's was one of them. Now, some people may have refused to ever take that country road again. That's one way to live. Or you can be like me. Tonight, I'm going to place my camping cot right under those icicles and fall asleep there. I'm not joking. I'm going to get my eight hours of slumber in the direct path of those spears and I'm going to sleep like a baby. Kids, you have to take on life with an attitude that says, I'm bigger than all of this. Otherwise, the world will beat you down till you're frightened bunnies."

Glen spoke loud enough for the people at the next booth to hear, and they now whispered to one another in that familiar way Rita and her brother had come to know so well.

"Dad, can you please keep your voice down," Rita begged, through clenched teeth. Her brother was staring at his plate, head in his hands, and Connie was angrily spooning mashed potatoes into her mouth.

"Does anyone around here even like winter?" Glen asked, eyebrows arched, mouth hanging open, as his knife and fork dropped to the tablecloth with a thud of punctuation. "What we're having this year is nothing, by the way. Let me tell you about winter when I was a kid..."

Rita excused herself to use the restroom, those at the next booth asked for their check, and Connie kicked Glen under the table, reminding him this was supposed to be Glen Junior's birthday party.

Lessons of March

"I like these cold, gray winter days. Days like these let you savor a bad mood."
— **Bill Watterson, creator of Calvin and Hobbes**

With apologies to T.S. Eliot, April is not the cruelest month. Not in the Northland. That title belongs to March. Winter is long, and even many of us who embrace it, and would feel its loss if it were not there on the calendar, know that by March it has served its purpose. We've had our winter. We've studied it, bathed in it, meditated on it, marveled at it, skied, skated, shoveled, scraped, slipped, shivered, and reveled in it. We have seen its tranquility, its rage, its mystery, its majesty, and we're ready for the next show, when the curtains open on blessed April.

Yet winter has more it wants to say. It's like the guest still talking near the doorway after a long evening. The meal was tasty and the conversation lively, but it's late, we're tired, and the guest has a coat on but isn't quite exiting. He or she has been reminded of one last story needing to be told, as the taxi idles in the driveway.

We're routinely saying our goodbyes to winter before it's ready to head down the road. And perhaps this is as it should be. Maybe the forces of the cosmos have offered us one final winter gift, if only we could see it that way.

Life is endless longing. How often are things not the way we'd prefer them, and how often do we wish for change? There is, perhaps, not a more succinct description of the human condition. Take away the longing for spring, and in its place put a neighborhood we want to move to but can't afford, or a part of the country we want to live in, but a job keeps us here. We imagine a more ideal relationship, a better boss, a prettier face, a happier disposition, a bigger salary. March takes us by the arm, sits us down, and says, "Calm down, kiddo."

In its gravelly voice, worn from the elements, it says, "Look out this window and just breathe. There I am, the last month of winter. I'm not here as tormentor. I'm the assisted living facility of a dying season. You don't think winter has much more to offer, I know. You've been with it since its youth, and you've watched it in all its adult glory. It has been your trusty companion, your whiny boss, your joyful playmate, your wise teacher, and your nagging neighbor. You feel you have taken all you can from it, and you wish to thank it and let it go. Yet it hangs on. And you say, wouldn't it be merciful if fate dispensed with it right now, clearing the way for an early spring?"

But March is asking us to shift. It calls on us to pivot from our longing to a more graceful acceptance. It's hard to fathom, but it's doing us an extraordinary favor. The mistake many of us make, however, is opting for resignation. Resignation can seem like acceptance, but it has more the flavor of surrender and defeat. March doesn't ask for that. Acceptance is a perspective shift, not a surrender. It stops the ache of grasping and relaxes the body. It moves us into the noticing of what is, not what ought to be. It removes outward reaching from the equation and replaces it with an inward seeing. And in that seeing there can be an appreciation for the miracle of life, in all its presentations.

The lessons of March can be taken anywhere. The old man at the care center sits beside his wife of 58 years. The summer lake cabin, the global travel, and the house full of children are all in the past now. But he looks at her frail body asleep in that bed and chooses to stop wishing for what was and instead feel the moment. What he feels is an exquisite love. By leaving the stories of the past or the hope for the future, a space is made for something larger. Something not directed by his wishes but directed at his soul. Room is made for the poignant, deeply felt mystery of human existence. A serenity descends, a quiet peace in the simple act of being alive.

When we fail to make room for these shifts, we're like the veteran ship captain steering his vessel through rough waters but never admiring the wonder of a roiling sea. With the acceptance of winter's pace in the natural cycle, the view out a March window on a gray slushy day is no longer something to wish away. It's life, created billions of years ago, an incomprehensibly complex phenomenon that we have tried to divide, corral, categorize, list, and label. In truth, there has never been a calendar, nor separated months. Nothing out there has a name. That's not how the world was delivered. It came wild. And it has never been tamed. March says, see my snow, my slush, my sleet, my winds, my gray. Know me. And then get ready. And here's where March offers its secret gift, one it rarely gets credit for. It intensifies the ecstasy of April, pumping it full of combustible energy. March takes spring's arrival from joyful pleasure to unbridled exaltation.

All intense experiences in life come in contrast to something else. Nothing is experienced in a vacuum. The thrill of a vacation comes after months on the job. The relief of a dive in a lake is born out of a sweltering day on land. And the longer and harsher the winter, the more welcome the spring. March adds four long weeks to a season that many were already prepared to send out the door. And then it clears the way for a season that should never have been given the same name it carries elsewhere in the country. Call it spring on the East Coast, West Coast, and in the South, but give the North another term for it, one that recognizes the transcendental sensation, spiritual infusion, energetic explosion, and ecstatic embrace. And thank March for amping up the impending bacchanalia.

But Northerners who heartily welcome spring can be teased and toyed with. Snow can appear to be packing its bags as the temps turn mild and pleasant. A window or two might be flung open for the first time in months as winter's flock begins the psychological shift to the new season. Then, suddenly, out of nowhere, the white flakes can return. And not just a few, but millions, one final winter blast. Cruel, some could argue. Yet, I've witnessed stout Northerners deliver the unexpected. "Ah, how lovely, one final look at winter in all her grandeur before she disappears entirely." Yes, I've witnessed gratitude. For the wise, there's the knowing that winter is returning for little more than a curtain call. It's like a last shower of sparkles in a summer firework display before the crowd folds up their lawn chairs. March is not being cruel. It's offering another great lesson. It's delivering its own Tibetan sand painting. Tibetan Buddhists have a long tradition of creating spectacularly complex geometric designs in colored sand. These mandalas are breathtaking works of art that rival preserved beauty in any museum. Yet, as soon as the massive, intricate masterpieces are completed and observed, they're wiped away. That act is meant to symbolically drive home the fleeting and transitory nature of the material world. We don't get to keep any of it for long. It's all in motion and passing us by.

For those who struggle with winter, that last winter storm, when spring was so close one could touch it, will be a letdown, a blow to a weary psyche. But if viewed as March's mandala, if seen as a masterful presentation of nature's intricate artwork, sure to vanish quickly and be replaced by something wholly different, one can accept and appreciate the ephemeral glory and impenetrable mystery. All is in flux. Let it be.

The Release

"If you think my winter is too cold, then you don't deserve my spring."
— **Erin Hanson, poet**

Years ago, I met a man who was traveling from Sweden on his summer vacation. We were discussing our country's respective differences, many of which were stark. But knowing he was a fellow Northerner, I steered the conversation to what I knew we had in common, winter. Instantly, we spoke the same language.

One exchange left us with the laughter of familiarity. We found we used the same event to mark the official arrival of spring. He said, "Is it your experience where you live that a day arrives when the street sweepers clear all the salt that has accumulated on the roadways, and when you see them coming down your street, you smile because you know it's truly over? They are taking the very last of winter from your neighborhood."

All he had to say was "street sweepers," and I immediately knew where he was going. Corny as it may sound, right then we bonded. It was as though he now lived next door, not across the ocean. We shared the ritual of watching an army of strange machines appear in our neighborhoods to literally sweep away the last of a season, as if having won a war.

But it didn't stop there. The Swede then asked if I also encountered a phenomenon on that first day in the spring when the shift in the seasons seemed most evident, when the air seemed unmistakably different, when the sound of the birds was almost triumphant, "where people on the street appeared intoxicated?" It was an apt description of Northerners in April, and I knew the experience well. More than knew it, I had felt it often. For me, it was a high distinct from any other known body and mind sensation.

The arrival of a Northern spring brings a seasonal delirium. One steps outside, and the air fails to deliver that bracing hello. The expectation of that chill against the cheek is countered by a gentle caress. It's soft and inviting, and some can tear up at the wonder of the contrast. Come April, Northerners have almost forgotten what that feels like. There is a newborn sweetness in the air, the scent of life telegraphing its jubilant return. The birds sound different. They're more of them, they're louder and clearer. The light touching everything seems to carry its own brand of emotion. Even the stoic trees seem aware of the shift, the frenetic squirrels move differently. One can sense all of existence delivering a cosmic exhale.

When I was a schoolboy, I would walk home on those first magnificent spring days imagining the sound of a symphony soaring high above neighborhood homes and echoing down residential streets. In my imagination, I would call upon all the dramatic music I'd ever heard in films or television shows, and I placed it in the air above me. The walk home demanded something exhilarating, a soundtrack as stirring and rhapsodic as the greatest scores I'd ever encountered. If I got the music just right, in my mind, I felt as though my heart were going to burst.

It's impossible to separate this depth of emotion from the season that has just passed. It's being born out of it, not arriving after it. The electrifying exhibition of spring is bursting out of the cracked shell of the long, cold dark. And not just in the external world, but deep inside most Northerners as well. The degree to which spring stands in contrast to the hard winter that has come before is often matched by the internal experience of those who have lived through it. The harder the winter, the greater the ecstasy. It is the last grand, gift-wrapped offering of the cold and the snow. It leaves Northerners with the kind of spring no one else in the country can claim. It's the reason the term "spring" in the North should be altered, perhaps presented in all capital letters.

With the arrival of spring, there will now be a new planet to walk upon, and it will gradually present a greater and greater abundance of burgeoning life in seemingly infinite variations. In twelve weeks, winter will seem all but incomprehensible to those escaping to the shade with a cold drink, wiping their sweaty brows with their shirt sleeves. But summer too will owe much of its lavish splendor to those foreign winter months. A Northerner's summer is celebrated for what it isn't as much as for what it is. Winter is so momentous, so weighty, it hovers over all the great seasons, a steady reminder of what they are not. It slumbers nearby in hibernation, patiently awaiting its turn in the cycle. For some, it waits as a haunting specter, ready to steal from us once more.

But winter has always given. From the beginning, it has given abundantly to all its hearty citizens, including its gift of our very identity. We are people of the North. We cannot separate ourselves from this lead actor in our annual four-act play. Its role in our world is too great, so great it scares many away. But for those who stay and come to know it, and know it deeply, it is a remarkably dynamic and enriching fellow traveler in our all-too-brief human lives.

About TD Mischke

TD Mischke is a writer, musician, podcaster, and former radio talk show host living in Saint Paul, Minnesota, where he was born and raised. He hosted The Mischke Broadcast at KSTP and WCCO radio in the Twin Cities for over two decades, and he was an award winning weekly columnist for City Pages, a Village Voice owned arts and alternative news publication based in Minneapolis. He's a piano player who has produced his own original recorded music, and he currently hosts The Mischke Roadshow (*mischkeroadshow.com*), a podcast featuring stories, interviews, insights, and observations from around the United States.

Acknowledgments

I got by with a little help from my friends, as I aways do in this world. My old pal, Ed Kemmick, deserves far more than heartfelt gratitude for being my editor. This wildly talented journalist is owed a hot buttered bourbon by a wood burning stove with a fiddle playing soft and sweet in the corner, as snow falls gently out the window. And my wonderful wife, Rosie O'Brien, a brilliant former book editor, has also earned a soft, comfortable chair near those sparkling flames. Her astute, insightful editing and style suggestions were invaluable. My dear friends, Jimmy Weinberg and Stephanie Volna, gifted graphic artists, get showered with loving praise for their help with the book cover design. Thank you both. And Wilson Webb, the highly accomplished camera cowboy who shot the back cover, I'll just say any photographer good enough to be a favorite of the Coen Brothers was probably too good for me. Thank you, Wilson.

I'll save one final tip of the cap for the one who helped raise me. That would be winter herself. Mama. I am a child of the North. Winter is in my bones, as it was in my father's before me on the Central Minnesota prairie, and as it was in his father's before him, on that same tundra, and his father's father's father, who built a little log shack there, in 1871, one that stills stands today. The American frontier was wide open back then, and yet when he crossed the sea, he chose the North to raise a family. That didn't make for an easy life in the 19th century, but then he wasn't aiming for easy. He had his sights on something else. Winter has coursed through the blood of his kin ever since, molding us as it sees fit. It doesn't make us better than anyone else. It just makes us different.

To learn more about
Skywater Publishing Cooperative
and our upcoming releases,
visit us at *https://skywaterpub.com*
or scan the QR code below.

Printed in the USA
CPSIA information can be obtained
at www.ICGtesting.com
JSHW080908061123
51314JS00001B/4